one hundred days of rain

one hundred

days of rain

carellin brooks

BOOKTHUG
DEPARTMENT OF NARRATIVE STUDIES
TORONTO, 2015

FIRST EDITION

Copyright © Carellin Brooks, 2015

The production of this book was made possible through the generous
assistance of the Canada Council for the Arts and the Ontario Arts
Council.

LIBRARY AND ARCHIVES CANADA CATALOGUING IN PUBLICATION

Brooks, Carellin, author
     One hundred days of rain / Carellin Brooks. -- First edition.

Issued in print and electronic formats.
ISBN 978-1-77166-090-7 (pbk.).--ISBN 978-1-77166-108-9 (html)

     I. Title.

PS8603.R6593O64 2015   C813'.6   C2015-900470-5
                                               C2015-900471-3

A **bundled** eBook edition is available
with the purchase of this print book.

CLEARLY PRINT YOUR NAME ABOVE IN UPPER CASE

Instructions to claim your eBook edition:
1. Download the BitLit app for Android or iOS
2. Write your name in **UPPER CASE** above
3. Use the BitLit app to submit a photo
4. Download your eBook to any device

PRINTED IN CANADA

After the neighbour calls the authorities. Reports the fight she overheard. Sets into motion the procedures for arrest and charge. The processes that will eventually bar our heroine from returning to her home. Then it begins to rain. She is not fallacious enough to connect this with her circumstances. She confines herself strictly to the facts. She leaves. It rains.

There's one thing, though. Despite how reliably it appears each day, the rain is never exactly the same. At one moment there might be a patter, as of little scrabbling squirrel paws on the roof; at another, a windblown torrent will fling itself against the panes of her room, rocking the window in its frame with sudden violence. She thinks that her own senses must deceive her. Surely there cannot be this many separate sorts of rain. But, as it turns out, there are.

1.

All of the noises of the jail are unfamiliar ones. She is surprised by how the procedures resemble those she's seen on TV, especially the invasive ones. Bend over, say the kindly impersonal guards - guards! - and she realizes, smiling disbelievingly, that they are serious.

Other things that she could not have predicted. The stamping of her hands, which are covered with rich black ink and pressed onto a special sheet, with sections. Everything has its place and is neatly organized: there's a sink afterwards, and a special kind of soap, to wash.

She poses for photos also, side and front, and at intervals is led to a telephone within a giant hood, like the sort of dryer they place over your head in an old-fashioned salon. When she picks up, at the end of the distant echoey line is a voice: a lawyer. There are two charges, two separate ritual calls, but his advice is invariable. What are you charged with?

he demands, at once, and when she tells him: Don't say anything. For he must know that she is bursting to talk to anyone who will listen: I am innocent, you are mistaken.

The heavy steps of the guards measure out the hallway beyond. There is the reassuring murmur of conversation and, behind that, a patter as of rain, dying slowly away with the distant clanging and clicking of doors closing, so faint that perhaps she has only imagined it. It was sunny when they took her, but hours have passed since then. Someone is screaming in another cell. At times the voice of a guard rises, shouting back. Someone in uniform brings her a bag: inside is an apple, a baloney sandwich, a box of milk. She drinks the milk, eats the apple. More hours pass. She is taken to the telephone again, shuffling, holding her blanket. They have given her a pair of jeans to wear, surprisingly decent ones, and taken away her shoes.

A justice of the peace is at the end of the line. He will release her but. She cannot return to her own home, own any knives but for cooking, contact her spouse. She questions these strictures. Perhaps, he suggests, she should wait and see a judge in the morning. No, that's fine, she murmurs hastily, the conditions are fine.

Now the opposite of what has come before: more forms to be completed, the ceremonial return of the belongings ceremonially removed upon her arrival. Your wife left you a message, the cop at the desk tells her as he hands back her purse. She says to call your psychiatrist, he's worried about

9

you. Oh, and she says she loves you. She notes, grimly, these misrepresentations. Says nothing. Who here has believed her so far, who cares?

She dresses again in the clothes of the morning: her dark grey woolen skirt, her pearls, a little cream crewneck sweater. Once again she dons her dead-black tights, and the thick wedge loafers. Her red coat with the blonde fur collar is a beacon, the sharp colour of love in a cartoon; her translucent purse nestles under her arm, a friendly ghost. Today might never have happened. Everything is as before but for the passage of time, and the stain on her, invisible to anyone else. Now you're sure you'll be okay? a female constable asks her anxiously, unlocking the door to the outside world. You don't want to call someone to pick you up? It's a rough neighbourhood, you know. Several replies occur to her but as with the message she stifles them. She has learned her lesson.

The rain tonight is her favourite kind: drops so widely spaced as to convince you, until one plops on your forehead or lands on your arm, that you are only imagining them. The sky appears clear but for a few drifting clouds: here on earth, a sudden dollop of liquid rides her skin before flattening and disappearing. A few raindrops speckle the pavement and the fabric expanse of her coat but the wet is indeterminate: at any moment it might stop or begin in earnest. She has always liked that, the uncertainty of it. Rain you can ignore, until it resolves itself into something else. The next morning is clear again.

2.

She has been left without the majority of her belongings now more than once. Careless, really. How does she find herself, she asks in her motel room, in these situations, with these people? The last man she dated, her son's father, went too. After he'd gone crazy she returned to her home to find it wrecked, everything sprayed and crushed and dribbled, a ruin. She fled to M and now this.

So, an accounting. A short one, for practically speaking she owns only what she carried away with her yesterday morning. A sturdy pair of shoes, ideal for walking, and a good thick coat. The wool sweater and skirt to keep her warm in all weathers. As if she'd planned it, this being left with what's on her back. They were fighting for days and nights. It went on and on with breaks. Maybe she knew.

Then the weather. Puffy clouds in an azure sky, as if they're in the tropics, as if it isn't still winter and near freezing outside. Brightness sparkles everywhere: on the carapaces of cars, on the metallic chips mixed into the concrete of a pair of giant planters outside the 7-Eleven she can see from her window, even on the rather dingy travellers, with their open guitar-cases, standing between them. Nobody has consulted her on the weather, she thinks with an air of injury only partly assumed. She would have preferred a lowered ceiling of leaden grey, the clouds swollen with their burden.

It's not all bad. Travelling soothes her and here she is travelling in her own city. Sometime she will have to call her friends and tell them what's happened. She puts off the task, unable to describe precisely this catastrophe. Once there, now here. Stunned, blinking. She will have to call her lover S in Seattle who has stuck by her all these years, a love partial and distanced, nonetheless surpassing all others. Maybe. Valentine's Day is coming. In her datebook she finds a postcard she meant to send S: a photograph of a pole at an intersection with two old-fashioned street signs. Love, they read, and Desire.

Looking again at the sky, she leaves her motel room a last time. Card in the box. The cheap motel room, like a photograph, a snapshot of everyone who's ever passed through. The place smells of old dry smoke, curling up from the walls. Its anonymity aggressive, in its own way. Saying: you know there'll be nothing left of you here, when you go.

3.

Manhattan and Vancouver have this in common: looking down an ordinary city street you see, at the end of it, empty sky. Go a little down one of these streets and discover that the sky belongs to water, a thin band of it shining flatly there, like a mirage.

When the rain comes this water that surrounds her city changes again. Grey and sullen but no less captivating for that, a pretty woman in a sulk. The sea comes in around the city, reaching cautious exploring fingers east: False Creek, Burrard Inlet, Indian Arm. Go out in a boat late in summer and see how salmon leap in the waters. Freighters loom higher than the land in the distance, a trick of perspective, giant shipping containers stacked up on their open decks like multicoloured blocks. Their bridges twelve stories high and stupid in their proportions, tall and thin like skyscrapers affixed to hulls. The men who work these ships enter the city only for short, unscheduled visits: hospital, police station, swimming pool (briefly). The newspaper prints a diagram, a cross-section of a container with its cargo of illegal immigrant. Stuffed toys, sneakers made in China. Nobody gets to go into the port. From afar you can see the orange-painted giant stackers, the lights that blaze all day, the road cresting a hump and then falling again, beyond, where it's impossible to see.

Along the edge of the bay is a path that skirts the shoreline. She has plenty of time to walk today. Her schedule with a hole in it, one she's fallen into, like Alice. The droplets today are fat, if as far between as those of the other night: sudden little explosions, unmistakable. They fall onto the walkers as if the cloud cover, strained to breaking by the effort of holding its watery suspension, has been unable to retain these lone harbingers. Rain like this an advance guard, warning of a squall to come. The raw wind sweeps in from the west. There, though they can't see them, are islands, and beyond that nothing, so they are told, until Japan. The wind buffets everything impartially: the water, the rocky shore, the few pedestrians she passes. It worries them and flings the drops into their exposed faces. She lowers her head and blinks, repelling the onslaught, caught. Go home it says. If she had one she would.

4.

It rained all the week before the day they got married. She was crossing her fingers. Praying even. For the wrong thing as it turned out. The sun finally came out that afternoon, just before time. She counted herself lucky. Thought it was a sign. They had their first argument on the way to the reception.

5.

All day rain continues to threaten. Dark overhang, mutter and threat. Weather in a temper. Something on its mind. Doesn't like to say. Clouds furrowed, roiling heavily overhead. Stirrings in a pot, coming to the boil. She goes to the giant thrift mart to augment her wardrobe. It is all very well to embrace the virtues of simplicity but a few days in one outfit is monotonous, even if you do carefully wash out your underthings each night in the sink.

She has never had much luck at this place, picked over as it is, but today she finds a short-sleeved red sweater and a pink-striped shirt that ties in the front with two bows. They can be worn separately, or one over the other. She stands in line behind the less fortunate, waiting to pay.

Outside the big front windows of the store rain has begun in earnest. This is the rain the denizens of the city know best, the rain they have cause to know. In the days before the weather began to change there would be weeks of it at a stretch. It is said of this rain that it drives people to suicide, that the sodden winter tries the strongest. Apocryphal tales are told of strangers who move to the city, seduced by summer's zephyrs, only to find themselves trapped in the grey world of the coldest months. If you're lucky there's a break in it, at Christmastime; if you are extremely lucky it snows. Otherwise the days without respite pile up: thirty-three in a row had been the record, thirty-three days of rain. Until now.

As for those who were born here rain is their birthright and she imagines that everyone expands just slightly under it, like mushrooms. They all have their different ways of coping. The mountains disappear. They like to drink tea and look out the windows, at least she does. They read newspapers and old novels. Newcomers scorn their ways. They drive harder in their piled-up trucks, headlights blazing, sheets of water parting for them. Mortgages to be paid, work to be done. Pedestrians leaping aside too late. The drivers don't even notice, heads tilted, hand to their jaws: a city of toothaches. Mumble. Astride her bicycle, she sets her teeth and follows in their wake. Her natural enemies, clearing a path.

Meanwhile the rain goes on, indifferent to their various responses. It is unvarying and monotonous: that's what drives the newcomers mad. No sound at all comes from it: no friendly patter or rattle of wind. The skies drip, that's all, and the relentless drip soaks silently into the land. She walks to the café to pick up her son. It's a long walk but she won't take the bus. Once again she is thankful for her thick-soled shoes. The misery of bad shoes, ones that let the weather in, so that your feet when you peel off your squishy socks have a pale, pinched look of reproach. She hopes her son will be wearing boots. The boy just turned five, practicality can't be expected of him. Did they have a party for him, before all this? They must have done but she can't recall. Everything from then turned grainy in her mind, everything except the fight with M receded as behind a screen, only the weather explicable. Only the physical left, to hold her up. Their belongings, inventory, survival, what they have and can see.

6.

The police, bless them, favour this café. They come in on their breaks, line up at the counter, drink lattes and eat muffins. Model citizens. They are there when she arrives, filling up two small tables in the middle of the room, weighted down like divers by belts studded with equipment. The child is with his father on a visit: they are expected in a few minutes. She waits, drinking milky coffee.

M, as she knew she would, arrives too. M looks just as usual: short pink face, the greying crewcut touched with darkness at the temples. The look of a small, surprised animal in the neat alert head and wide-set ears. Her usual outfit: button-down, khakis, pull-on Australian boots. M affects surprise. What on earth is she doing here, M wonders aloud. M decides that if she wants to say hello to her child it's fine. She stares stolidly at a point on the wall. Then the lights of the car belonging to her child's father, sliding across the far wall of the café as it turns in. She stands up and walks to the table full of officers.

Excuse me, she says. This woman, pointing to M, insists on speaking to me.

The officers show no surprise. Two of them stand up, lead the women separately to the thin strip of sidewalk outside the café. It has begun to rain again: she can see the widely spaced dashes on the concrete. A spotty, insinuating rain, an irritant. The voices of the officers as they ask their questions are low, intimate. Words bubble: psychiatrist, assault, restraining order. A third policeman intercepts her child's father as he stands up from the inside of the car. There were scenes like this, worse in fact, in her own childhood: shrieking adults in the driveway, cars and parents coming and going. Never again, she swore.

What is going on? the child's father demands, striding at last into the cafe. Darkness has fallen, the windows to the outside turned glossy slate. The police have cleared out. Even M has gone. Only she and the child remain, survivors on a raft, fortifying themselves with hot sweet drinks.

There's been a bit of a . . . She hesitates delicately. Now that it is all over, now that she has her child by her, she feels faint, like a heroine of olden times.

Apparently you've been acting crazy? You look pretty sane to me. Ah, sanity. Such a subjective opinion. He's the one who went last time around. She recollects her shattered apartment, his words of rage. Now here he is, confirming her soundness of mind. She's even grateful. Imagine that.

7.

They take refuge. It's a modest building downtown, on Barclay Street. Their sixth-floor corner apartment studded with Air Wick fresheners but she fixes that. The heat is always on. A boon given their meagre wardrobes. They're camping out. At least life is simple, she says.

Let's make everything normal.

Let's pretend like nothing bad happened.

Her child wants to call M. Why not. Because M will recognize the number, know where they are. M will call the landlord, who she happens to know. An acquaintance of theirs. Concerned, she'll be. Just thought you should know.

Sure, go ahead. Of course. Her child's treble. Outside, the rain continues. From the sixth floor the sky behind the building opposite (stained stucco, faux-cheerful iron tubing in primary red) is a featureless pale grey, undifferentiated even to the extent of clouds. There is no way to tell it's actually raining: the drops themselves are invisible both in the air, as they fall, and on the ground. Only the continuing darkness of the pavements below explains.

You never get wet in this sort of rain: you never get dry either. The state is an interstice, an amphibious aquatic one. She can see the people outside, on the sidewalk below. They scuttle along with their heads bowed. A whole city of penitents, praying. She knows what they want & need and for what they yearn.

They pray for the clouds to lift.

They pray to see the sun again, however briefly, even once. The sun to them a precious object each person has at some time wandered away from, absently, taking it for granted. Has casually saluted: Oh hi. You again.

Never again. This time I'll. But who will believe them, now?

Sometimes they are given a chance. There is a part of the day, hours after they leave the apartment on Barclay Street, when she receives her allotment. For whole minutes a shaft of sunlight will reach directly into the alleyway behind the building where she works. Their lane an empty bowl filling up with bright. On the way home, framed by the window of the bus, the sun shows itself in the sky above. It's a kind of sleight of hand, the gleaming silver coin winking in the magician's grasp. Then vanished, and the grey curdled over once again. The trick.

There is a jogging track on the low roof of the next building, a rust-coloured oval, dark with moisture, that nobody ever uses. Across the street the red metal railings, turned over the stained frontage of the facing building. Everything built in the past two decades holds the wet. This sort of construction, with its stucco cladding, nobody considered ruinous at first, nobody questioned it. The processes were internal and invisible: for years everybody would have said everything was fine, nothing had changed. There was no excuse for this really: everyone was familiar with the rain, its duration and persistence. Then the walls began to sag and they opened them up and found the rot.

There's an old man in the elevator one day as they come back from their errands, a cheery, sprightly fellow. He has gleaming eyes and springy white hair and if he looks a little grey around the edges so do they all, in the rain.

He begins to tell her about his wife who died in hospital nearby. I've been here since the building was built, he tells them. In 1962.

He probably tells everybody that, in the elevator.

8.

They move to her friend Trouble's apartment in a four-storey stucco complex off a main street where the traffic never stops. Trouble is away for a week and says she is welcome to use the place in her absence. Her lover S comes to visit from Seattle that night. The next day M picks up the child for a visit. It's another anniversary, the day they met, although neither of them feels much like celebrating, now.

Instead she and S spend the day cleaning. S gets down on her hands and knees and scrubs at the oily black smears on the linoleum with a toothbrush. When evening comes M phones. M says she will not give her son back. They drive to the verge of the road a block away from her former home, as close as she is allowed. Pull the borrowed car over to the side. Overhead the hammered sky. Shifting grumbles. A muttered threat. A few drops fall and hang there on the car's curved windshield. The angles all wrong. The speckled sign of rain suspended above.

The police come. She sees so much of the police lately. The social workers too. Seems her reputation precedes her, however unearned. They accuse her of being in unsatisfactory surroundings. They accuse her of not having the child's best interests at heart. They threaten her with foster homes. Is this what you want for your child they say.

Eventually, grudgingly, someone consents to inspect her accommodations. They are pronounced adequate. Can she get her boy now then. Not possible, the social workers point out smugly. Her child has gone to bed hours ago, in M's house. Surely she would not be so cruel as to disturb him.

The weather holds, as she and S see the skilled helping professionals to the door. Beyond the breezeway it is almost quiet, but for the sigh of cars passing. No torrent. No drenching. No downpour. The sky has turned black.

9.

The squall that has threatened for days finally breaks. The rain comes in sudden savage bursts. Drops fling themselves at the unprotected faces of pedestrians, sliding sideways under umbrellas and hoods. There is an angry pattering insistence to the tattoo. Their weather is on the march. No more of these sullen sodden half-measures. A mother in a tantrum, the rain exhorts them with angry exclamations. Get busy! Get going! Clean this mess up right now!

They get into the swing of things. They match storm's rhythm. They pick their feet up in the eddying swirls of water that rush for the drains. They stomp and splash in galoshes and boots. They resign themselves to wet socks. Their pants are wicks. Hair under their caps catches rain and curls from it.

On the way to work, lunch must be found for her and her son both. Her native frugality warring against the necessity of buying them readymade. And then the child is so very difficult. How about this. No. How about this. Not that. What then, for the love of God. I can't go on looking forever, she says. You like pasta. Try pasta salad. Knowing he won't. That the salad will come back untouched, inevitable, a reproach.

They buy Pellegrino in little bottles. She half-fills the empties with milk. This she can do. The child confiding on their walk to preschool: I tell the teacher I drink beer.

She halts. Visions of the social workers. Why? Why would you do that? It's not beer.

The child shrugs, nonchalant. I know. I just like to pretend.

At work she coaxes herself like an invalid, small portions at intervals. It all goes. She eats a lot of yogurt. It doesn't help. She knows that she is pining, as she sits staring out at the storm. She reminds weather that it is she who is inside, trapped, but rain still slaps at the glass, demanding to be let out or in, demanding that nothing be put in its way.

10.

The next day puddles hopscotch the sidewalks. Some of them stretch the whole way across, others shrink timidly from contact with the green. Her little son hops from wet to wet. Splashes add to the general ruination. The rain has settled at least. There is a gentle strafing on the multiple surfaces of water, nothing more.

Her lover S comes to visit. For two nights they take a room in a hotel. That night they sit in the bar, drinking, while her son sleeps in the room upstairs. There's a street outside, running under their room, and on the right-hand side of the hotel a sort of cobbled courtyard, made out of a section of street taken up and given over to pedestrians. At one point this part of the downtown was a veritable open-air prostitutes' mart, and in response the city created all sorts of one-ways and dead-ends, so that you drive through them backtracking and detouring in maze fashion. The rain falls lightly against the leaves of the trees and shrubs put in to enhance the park-like effect. They can hear it, faintly, from where they sit at the bar. She eddies the ice cubes in her glass in pale sympathy and the bartender looks up alertly to ask if she wants another.

S says very little. There is little to say. S will of course be back, as she was after the child's birth, to help for the enormous work to come. The extracting of the belongings, and the moving, and the dealing with the police, and the days in court that might follow. In between S will return to her own city and thank her lucky stars for distance. But there's nothing they can do now, as the child tosses in one of the big beds upstairs.

In the morning there's a bust across the street. A police cruiser is pulled in to the curb and a skinny, dirty fellow half-lies against it, his arms fastened behind him. The sun has come out again. The light it affords is watery, a warning of impermanence. On the sidewalk the officers stand around, conversing in desultory fashion. She watches them from behind her gauzy nylon curtain. Until recently her sympathies would have been all with the forces of law. Nowadays she is less certain. She glances up at the sky. A few clouds drifting. The weather holds.

11.

The first apartment she's shown in the red-brick building is on the sixth floor. It's a sunny day and the park spreads out below her from two windows. The current tenant has sensibly restricted (himself? herself?) to a single piece of furniture: a giant futon cantilevered into a couch, with wheels set to stay and a robust corduroy cover. She falls in love at once.

That one's gone, says the harried building manager when he calls her later with good news. She has been accepted & approved. He's tall and Slavic, this manager, with an indeterminate accent, probably from a vanished country. He has an erect brush of brown hair and is one of those men whose tone comes entirely from their circumstances. He could be kind, he could be cruel, all with the same lack of thought, no flicker to animate those small dark eyes. There is one on the first floor available, he continues.

It's evening when she goes back. Her son alone in their temporary apartment a block away. It may not be true anymore that they don't rent to people with children but she can't be sure. She can't take anything for granted.

The first-floor apartment is supposed to be a clone of the one on the sixth floor but to her eyes they are entirely different. Boxes and belongings clutter the dim dingy room. The pullout bed a cavern. Outside a swishing and sighing, faint. It is too close, there in the room, to tell if she is listening to the rain, brushing against the windows, or the cars that rush ceaselessly on the road outside.

The next day she calls back with renter's remorse. It's too dark, she says over and over. The Slavic manager deals more kindly with her than she might have expected, talks her into it in fact. She tells herself they can always move.

12.

On the day she is to pick up her belongings she rents a van, the smallest one she can get, and still backs into another car in the drugstore parking lot. A stranger has to talk her off the other car's bumper, which he does, sensibly and without fuss.

She drives to the café near her and M's house. Calls the police who must accompany her given her apparently terrible ways. The police are busy. She waits and calls back, waits and calls back. Finally the police call her. M has refused, they say. She will have to come another day. But the van, the empty apartment. Her son. In vain she argues.

She has to call her son's father. It's the second time they've spoken in years, after the night with the police at the other café. He arrives in an hour. Foam mattress, bucket, soap, cups & dishes. Sheets & towels. Drives her to the store for a clock and dishpan. Returns the van for her, drives them both back downtown. Large & silent in the driver's seat. Her son asks nothing. Why are we moving. Why don't we have our things. What will happen to us.

13.

Their new apartment is too cold, the weather has turned and suddenly she's wearing wool which seems a little excessive. The rain streaks the angled glass roof across from her windows. Each day these panes are her barometer. Today the drops form an indeterminate scree, silvery streaks veining the steep pitch. Someone upstairs is walking restless as her, her slow dragging steps echoed there, in counterpoint.

She forces herself to go outside. In this mood only force works. People on the sidewalk are breathing like smokers, each wet puff overloading the already supersaturated atmosphere. She should care, believe, something, whatever. Add her mite. Anything but this dull grey cloud over everything, suffocating her.

14.

The child's father has her son for the week. Alone she wakes to rain, seeping into crevices all around. She imagines she can hear it on the roof, five storeys above. Each storey a layer of people, like a cake studded with fruit. The rain coming through them all, through her. There must have been a time when the sun shone however watery. When the clouds parted and that single weak ray made its unerring way to ground. The point of God's finger. But the wet world has wrapped her too long, she no longer remembers anything else. Rain has worked its way into a permanent condition.

She locks up the dim room where she lives. Outside the sky an undifferentiated lowering mass. There is no dark or light, just this pressing pale grey like an iron held up against the city. Blunt & inarguable against the constructed world. Steaming. Pedestrians cross the street without looking up.

Rain continues. It's there every time she glances out her window at work, the one window permitted in their jail cell of a barred interior. Rain when she steps to the alley door to take a breather. Rain when she mounts her cycle. Well, bye then, she says to her coworkers, and rings her bell. Her bell unanswered in the alley. No need to hurry, with no child to pick up. She pedals down the wet road. Vehicle headlights flash as they turn before her in the pre-dusk gloom. More and more she takes her hands off the bars, more and more she's able to balance unaided. Folly, this sense of effortless motion on the rain-slick street.

The rain continues. February, month of love, drugstore hearts and gas-station flowers. Her son's birthday, past now, her (deceased) grandmother's birthday, her lover S's birthday. People to think about. No point putting cards in the mail, buying presents. Not this year.

The weekend comes. The child hers again. S back in town, S who comes to visit regularly and faithfully, nine years now. They are watching the game in the restaurant, she and S and the child. Okay S is watching. Plates & pints. What normal people do. She clings to it. On TV the rain is invisible. The football teams catch & fumble, drops spatter the lens. The camera pulls away and the rain is suddenly central to it all, visible, Biblical, coming down like fury on the people in the stadium. Helpless. The ball goes up again, arcing in that particular irregular parabola, the football players' sinewy delicate hands reaching and failing to grasp.

15.

Rain overwhelms her as she plods from foot to foot. The kind of rain that can't be ignored. It envelops her, it makes even walking to the corner a misery. Each drop weighs in, another small burden, and the splashes coming up from under make it impossible to stay dry. There hasn't been a kind of covering invented that works. People with umbrellas duck under the overhang, everyone threading their way from shelter to shelter on the dark street. There was a dawn, hours ago, and hours from now there will be a sunset, so she's told or remembers from long ago. Meanwhile this obliterating rain obscures everything. The luckiest maddest ones are swathed in coats, hoods pulled up over their faces, pants of rainproof drip-dry material. They move through the world as through an alien landscape, astronauts, swaddled & untouchable.

Rainproof. Like quick and easy weight loss, a demonstrable lie.

S is visiting again. S wants to know if she possesses an umbrella. As if. Her son dressed in fire-licked rubber boots with little eyes. They are all miserable as they trudge from place to place. Should we take the bus. Yes, yes, pipes the little one, sodden. The adults grudging the cost.

All the time now she makes mistakes. The next morning she forgets her wallet. Let me off, she says to the driver. Last week they were on their way to school in the rain, she and her child, when the driver stopped the bus with a jerk. The child somersaulted head over heels down the aisle. She came stomping up to the front to complain, her son in her arms wailing. Would you stop driving that way, she hissed.

I didn't do anything. The wail impossible to ignore, he capitulated grudgingly. Okay, okay, I'm sorry.

So she doesn't expect mercy today. But he says it's fine, waves a hand. Settle up with me later. She sits back down, indignation leaking from her pricked. Unfamiliar, this curdling mix of outrage and gratitude. Outside the windows, what else, rain.

16.

From inside the windows of the bus the passengers watch rain. Condensation wraps them in a frosted blanket of glass. She smears herself a hole to look out. Outside is the same view as always, the wet darkened streets, the unlucky. They totter from place to place trailing blankets. They shamble heedless across the avenue. The bus she's on slows and picks up speed and stops regretfully a safe block from Chinatown's main intersection. The Chinese crowd on. There is a lot of excited conversation over who's to sit where. Maybe something else. The bus begins to move again, the hesitant lurch and rush of the bus. Everyone falls silent, clutching plastic bags.

They are going to work to school. They are going going beyond the reach of rain. They won't be caught. They won't be left out. Rain is a vengeful thing, it has but one goal. To saturate them. Rain would like to fill her up until she can't hold it in any more. She sees herself broken and flooding, a vessel. She knows they should feel grateful to rain that fills up the city's reservoirs for summer. That waters the bushes & grass so that they spring up later. They're impatient though. It's difficult to grasp, to think ahead. Theoretical. What matters is the here & now. Rain is the citizenry's inheritance, their boondoggle, their folly, their insurance policy. Rain creates. Rain is cause and effect. Rain makes them.

17.

Vancouver, on the edge of the rain forest, the mountains a craggy wall. They are friendly and they stop the weather cold so that rain stays. The sea too does its part. Buffeted here between wet expanse and high back. Nothing else suits her, not the high or wide plain, not the anonymous inland tuck of cities in the smack centre of big islands. Without mountains at her back and sea at her feet she feels unmoored, drifting. Take me and keep me. Never let me go.

There are other places, true. Places she stayed and about which she can testify upon returning that it never rained there, not once. Kingston. The cold knife-like, that sharp it was. Summers muggy & clear. Quebec City, her lashes freezing together, the warm sweep of her uncovered shoulder above the woolen sweater when she took off her coat. All the students wore giant overcoats from the thrift store, boiled wool, heavy as God the Father.

It never rained in New York City either. How she begged for rain as that summer stretched out. To wash the pee away. So many men peed in the streets, there was nothing else you could do if you didn't have a toilet. She wanted rain to overlay the smells, smells that climbed and inter-twined as day after day the heat continued to lengthen and rise. She walked through not grimacing, shuddering inside.

18.

Places she lived where it did rain. A different kind of rain though. In Salt Lake City the storms came sudden out of the west. One minute cloudless ordinary sky. The unthreatening sky of the desert. The next rain had passed over in violence. There was a hard insistent quality to the way it dropped on them, for twenty minutes or so. The colour of the rain was yellow. It threw up the dust as it hit. She could watch the rain from under overhangs where everybody dashed. In a few minutes it was gone again and the mountains, mauve in the distance, resumed their indifferent overlooking. The rain was like a murky dream that came and passed. She had imagined it perhaps. Given another hour the pavements resumed their colouring of bone, the moisture bleached clean from them.

19.

In Birmingham it rained just like home except nobody mentioned it, nobody seemed to think it worthy of notice. The rain went on and on and on, dreary, dripping, like a man with a head cold and not enough energy to wipe his nose. It was too pervasive to be discussed. It lasted too long. It took the heart and spirit out of them. The locals found themselves in pubs drinking beer. Lager. Mild. Bitter. Something to quench the spark the rain had almost, but not quite, succeeded in putting out.

Later everybody got on the bus damp and drunk and it didn't matter any more.

20.

She cycles in the wet, in the thick of it. Her pants dampen, then go slack, pulling away from the lean flesh of her legs: sand clings to their bottoms. Why sand? It's what lies on the street, arcs under her wheels. Her bicycle is dirty - so dirty she should clean it, instead of letting it sully the interiors of kind strangers' cars. She will cycle again today. Again today it is raining. Cycling in the rain: proof of her stoicism, what sort of person she is. What she's earned and deserves. How good she is.

Yesterday she saw a film about cyclists in Vancouver. They were cycling over the Lion's Gate Bridge, which goes straight up. Swarming against the dark pavement like crawling insects on a hill. How ugly they looked swathed in their outdoor jackets, their helmet covers like puffy mushrooms. How grey the world was. How brave they were, braving rain. There is something perverse about them all, or must be, to choose this. To resist what is comfortable. To exercise their rights. To be wet, and ultimately to be wrong.

21.

Weekly her son visits M. The child returns the next day bearing twists of cookies in a small stack, chocolate-covered raisins. Darkening pears. M phones in a flutter: I had no idea his teeth were so bad. This after the second set of cavities. The child isn't allowed any of the sugary snacks and his mother will touch none of the fruit, not if it's the last piece in the bowl.

A few days ago the drinks cupboard was bare and she persuaded herself to a can of soda the child had toted all the way from M's place. It's sealed, she told herself, it's not as if it could possibly hurt me. She drank it down and the acid rose in her throat in a terrible boil.

Yesterday she was in a courtroom with M, M's lawyer, a judge. A friendly meeting, supposedly. A chance to work things out although she would testify M has no such intention. The judge makes the customary speech about the harm done children by warring spouses. M nods, puts on her sincere expression. Later M screams that her son is confused: he doesn't understand why his mother is returning all the gifts M ever gave her. With some pleasure she is able to inquire mildly as to how her child comes to know of such things. M falls silent.

Today rain is a faint stippling on the glass across the way, sun illuminating each drop so that it stands out in glorious relief. Today the rain invites ignoring, persuading her almost, as she glances out her window, that it's not really there. Don't bother with a coat, a hat, an all-encompassing rainsuit: it's February after all. Nearly spring.

Outside, rain is a trace, the sky rising brilliant above. The wet streets on which she walks seem almost impossible, the drops scattered on every surface illusory. Surely there has been no rain, not on such a fine day as this. Surely everyone's very eyes and nostrils are mistaken.

22.

Once more rain has come back, faithless unwelcome friend. Bad penny. Everyone bumping around outside like the invitees in the hallway of a party that isn't going. Slowly fighting to get out. Avoiding rain's gaze. Rain doesn't seem to notice. Once more rain coats the glass with tiny bumps and rivulets. Once more rain nyah-nyahs her with the damp of its embrace, to forsake shelter, to brave rain. How she will come home smelling of the wet, how gradually her things will dry, how squelchy and generally mussed she will feel: only she knows these things. Rain has no conscience, it thinks of nothing now or ever beyond the wet earth and always down, down, into and inside. Rain is inexorable and dumb, it can't even speak except in a tiny drumming.

Yesterday it seemed rain had gone for good. How bravely the sun shone, how careless were the few clouds in the sky. Us? Harmless, we tell you. And she believed it, they were so fluffy and light, like pancakes.

Her city is a rainless one, it will always shine on her this way: these are the kind of lies she believes when the sun spreads out with such rich abandon. She's good at forgetting, not remembering. A survival skill, maybe. Yesterday she wandered the shopping street near her place in a half-daze, meeting nobody's eye. Clothes in brilliant windows, fancy magazines with bright covers, and the pedestrians, a little out of place in all the gleam. The women not quite right in some way, their clothes too old, their faces too fat, their expressions peevish or distracted. All passing under her indifferent undifferentiating gaze.

This morning she gets up and oils her boots. The leather gradually darkens, the creases turn almost black, the scuffed tops take on a sheen. They will be proof against anything: puddles, infidelity, mutual accusations, even her private and wild despair. She developed a passion for these boots in the store, even though – or perhaps because – they are like nothing else she owns. They were outdoorsy and pretend-rugged: they reminded her of starlets gamely trekking wilderness trails for photos. There was a fey, almost girlish quality to the two buckled straps at top and bottom, despite the gesture towards practicality in the stacked wooden heels. Yesterday she was getting dressed when Nurse phoned. She had nothing on but the boots over a pair of socks. She stood and talked to Nurse, who she's dating in desultory fashion, and sorted through receipts, looking at herself in the mirror all the while. Monstrous self-satisfaction. When rain next comes she will be ready.

23.

The smell of rain is ozone, smoke, earth, and cloud: a smell impossible to duplicate or bottle, though people try. "Spring Rain"-scented detergent. "Summer Rain" cologne.

"Winter Rain": disinterred ski suits, mildew, urine and chill.

"Autumn Rain": clouds of leaves left to moulder on the ground, skunk spray in the park, a sharp overtone of dog waste.

Springtime. Find a field, a park will do, and one of those days that cries out with the promise of it. Smell the green. Listen to the soft patter across the grass like tiny rabbits running away from you. Run with rain. No coat.

Wait until summer. Night falls, later than anyone could imagine. The rain starts up again as if it has been waiting for this: a soft insistent patter, gentle as faith. Looking out into the night there is no way to believe in rain, invisible.

Go out to the nearest body of water in which it is permissible to bathe, or more practically one with a low fence. Go out to the sea.

It should be high summer. August, when the heat is at its peak, when you pant a little just breathing, when exertion seems unthinkable. When you are covered with your own moisture, visibly. When you wait for night like the answer to a wish.

Slip into the water, the ocean, the salt: slip into the warm liquid from whence we are rumoured to have come. The ocean and the air are practically the same temperature: it's like floating in a cool bathtub.

Turn on your back, let yourself float belly-up, let the rain cover you with little x's.

Of course take off all your clothes.

Watch autumn rain from behind a window, warm cup in your hands. Curl in the frame of the window if possible. Wear your most touchable clothes, the loosely woven chunky sweater, the velveteen pull-on pants. Wear woolen socks that don't itch. Feel your feet in them.

In winter wish for snow.

24.

This morning rain is faint, almost Victorian. Rain totters about with a skim-milk wrist held to its forehead, collapses on the divan. Rain seems not to be long for this world.

Outside the cars swish on by, ignoring rain, the possibility of it, the outside world. Who cares! Rain has nothing on them. Rain can't get in behind these sealed windows. Rain is barely there, not worth noticing, another dismissable part of the world nobody quite inhabits anymore.

Rain's days are numbered, it seems. The way rain does things is not the way things are done, not any longer. Rain doesn't have any interface, it isn't mediated. It lies there shuddering. Not very long now, rain murmurs quietly to itself.

25.

In Victoria overnight to attend a conference, she emerges onto wet streets in the morning. There is no sign of rain. The city's ordinary residents seem unastonished by this. So far as she can tell their normal temper, a mild ever-present sweetness, remains unchanged. They live in a slower simpler town. Not so much of this hurry hurry and let's go. Everyone has umbrellas and hats at the ready of course, that's the kind of place it is. But there's no need. Rain has vanished from above the quiet city, leaving only the evidence of its passage: a stain, to fade in turn.

A different kind of wet awaits as the ferry pulls itself towards Vancouver. Another ship draws close, displaying an enormous confidence. Giant and balletic, the white boats pivot around an invisible central axis, toot their mournful whistles one to the other. This is the narrowest part of the passage, here between these rocky islands with their houses levered out from the slope, above the meagre skirts of sands.

Ahead rain gathers on the slopes of the nearer islands. You can't see rain until you draw closer, into its midst. The clouds thicken into a white concentration in the folds of the hills rising sternly in their turn from the mist.

In Vancouver the sun is a sudden shining, a punchline. She turns her face up to it: brevity, and the bright quaver of the light.

26.

Heading out into the shrouded afternoon rain has oblit-
erated all else. Heavy, wet drops cover the known world.
They are splashing like a curtain wrapped around her as
she bicycles with her head down.

In a few seconds she feels the wetness trickling into her
shoes. Her face all slick. Plastered to her is the hair that
creeps out from under her helmet. She thinks she can feel
rain working its way into the vents above her head. Rain
is coldly furious. It finds the hidden ways inside coat &
covering, seeping through to the tender skin of her neck.
Her scalp.

She arrives at the office drenched. Her tights heavy at their
bottoms with trapped moisture. She takes off her soaked
shoes under the table where nobody can see. Her dripping
black overcoat. There is nowhere to hang it so she settles
for the back of her chair. The arms of the silk shantung

jacket she picked out this morning before school are bleeding at the insides of the elbows. Dusty rose blooming a shocked pink. She takes that off too - she has to - and hangs it discreetly from her chair's arm. The chill settles in. This is what is worst about rain: the getting inside, the wet left on her. She is stained by her journey, short as it was: the marks of passage are upon her. It is all very well to say that she will dry but what nobody counts are these silent dripping hours in between, and the shiver. Rain has ruined her.

27.

In the years she and M lived together their duplex was on the southern edge of the city. She wrote grants for the arts consortium that rented out space from the university. Working mostly at her computer. Occasional days she visited.

She and M lived at the top of a hill. You could see weather coming, clouds in the far sky or wisping round the mountains, and the brown smudge that blurred the hills across the way. On a bicycle you were in it for the long haul, unless she called on M's near-vintage Land Rover. It looked all right that day. She decided to ride to the campus, a good hour away on the perimeter road.

On her way back from the university, the weather shifted. Morning's clear skies vanished. The sky turned dark, then let loose. Water fell on her unceasingly, as from a bucket. The streets were slick. A mist before her eyes made it difficult to see. A passing bus threw up a watery frill between her and the road. This is crazy, she thought. Shivering in her suit and overcoat, she pulled over.

M was home. So you want me to drop everything and come get you.

Yes.

Well I won't. If you cared about what I have to do, you wouldn't even ask.

She was so tired when she dragged herself in the back door finally, like a warrior returning from a great battle. Too tired to feel anything. When she took off her coat she saw that the furious rain had leached through to her clothes below. There was a fat spreading line down the centre of her back, where she had hunched over the handlebars. The sleeves of her fine woolen suit wet up to the middle of her forearms, as if she'd plunged them in water. Her brown hair, grown only as far as her neck then, soaked.

You think I wasn't there for you but that's not true, M told her later. They were having one of their fights. She was bringing up things from the past that still bothered her, which you weren't supposed to do. At that time in her life she read books about relationships, the kind of books she'd always scorned, and tried to follow their precepts. "I" statements. Sticking to the issue. Times she felt like a counselor herself.

Later she thought M must resent her knowledge. How she remembered, might always remember, hanging on the line and being told no.

28.

Rain again. Dismayed she goes to the office door. The alley is awash, the pigeons who gather on the asphalt vanished. Their feed lies sodden on the tiny-trampled ground of the neighbour's backyard. He only does it to annoy.

The grass has a hopeful spring look, rising in rain's dark. Its green is almost luminous, in the murky day.

She would like to deny rain, its very existence. Or if it can't be denied, to say it's not so bad.

She would like to defy rain. To lift a fist and challenge rain: do your worst!

She would like most of all for rain not to touch her. But even she knows she can't seal herself off completely. She reminds herself, like a catechism you recite: it's not so bad.

You'll feel better once you're out in it. You'll warm up. You'll see.

Shivering, unwilling, full of disbelief, she mounts her cycle. On the ride what she has promised comes slowly true. The miracle. By the time she arrives home she is so flushed and rosy from her exertions that when she shrugs off her black coat she imagines herself steaming. So deeply warm that she can no longer even feel rain on her.

29.

The colour of rain is the very shade of negation. More than anything, rain declares solemnly: I do not exist.

Ignore me. Really. Don't disturb yourself.

As if she ever could, she thinks. As if she can pretend it's not there, go on as usual. No matter the camouflage colours into which rain considerately shades itself: grey, blue, a kind of pale undersided green like the belly of a floating fish.

Sometimes rain looks a mirror in the dark, each tiny dropping facet another reflection of what can't be seen. Sometimes rain grades infinite greys so that there is no near, no far, only what falls between her and them. Sometimes rain winks out the distance. Sometimes rain really is invisible.

30.

Tomorrow's deadline looms. She must list all her assets and debt. Estimate her spending on shampoo and conditioner. Add up the magazines. Cost out the price of gifts over a twelve-month period. Indicate her savings. Afterwards she is required to submit: an examiner, a judge. There is a building set aside for the purpose and she trembles to enter it.

Rather than hunched over her table, cudgeling her brains, she prefers to be outside where paper is an impossibility. Here are no receipts and half-remembered purchases, only the stores they were taken from, their windows square behind the ceaseless falling of rain.

She has no hat, no umbrella. Bareheaded she goes out into rain. Her hair takes the brunt of the weather, the brown deepening again to black as it twists imperceptibly into rope. Under its protection she hardly registers rain's steady fall. Then a large wet plop falls on her head, soaking through, and lays a cold fingertip on her very scalp. She shudders, scowling, and shakes herself like a dog. Then hurries on.

31.

M calls and asks to speak to the child.

She says stiffly that her child is not with her.

M's voice hesitant, carefully correct.

Rain pummels tiny fists on the window. Tinkles and dances, a small drumming like fingers on a tabletop. Rain gusts and smatters against the glass, pushed by wind. She imagines herself reaching through the phone cord, along the wires, to change that voice to something gasping and frightened. A desire so vivid she feels her hands clutching, the strain of the tendons.

She would like the voice to go away, so that she never has to hear it again in her life.

M calls again the next night and asks for her son.

Again she says the child is not there.

M calls and asks for her child.

By nightfall the sound of rain has died away. Outside, as she hurries down the street in tippy-tippy heels, her feet bent nearly perpendicular or so it feels, she hears nothing at all. The only way she can tell that rain is still with her and not gone away again is the darkening deepening wet of the streets, under streetlights and traffic lights and before the shining fronts of shops. Rain a man waiting around the corner. Shadow, breath. Following something or someone. Black and white.

She enters a building, goes into an auditorium. She has been invited to read from her work in progress. The sound of her own voice, when she mounts the stage, loud and comforting. She uses it like a caress and whisper. Rain has taught her that at least, how to speak.

32.

Why take a bath when it is raining? Why run the water and step in, and then step out again and carefully towel yourself off? Why powder between your toes, wrap another towel tightly around your head, stay inside until your hair is dry, or if you have to go out at once wield the blow dryer?

This morning rain stipples the glass of the overhang opposite, a faintly traced promise. Last night, when she wheeled her bicycle out her office door, the sky had lowered to just above the tops of buildings. The clouds were not their usual almost-raining colour: a pale and uninteresting grey, like mother-of-pearl without the gleam. Instead they had darkened to the colour of slate. The sky sat on the housetops like a headache or bad news from another country. A few stray drops fell on her as she cycled home: at any moment she expected the deluge. But for hours the rain remained stalled, a needle poised above revolving vinyl. Carrying the heavy bag of magazines to her friend Trouble's car she felt it at last, but not the storm she'd been expecting. Instead the rain beat a faint needlelike tattoo on her bare arms and uncovered head. She handed off the parcels hurriedly before running back inside.

This week she is childless. Dinners of dollar pizza slices or Vietnamese subs. No point in cooking. The fruit bowl empty. She works longer hours, goes out at night, stays up late and sleeps in. Always this ache plucking at her, chronic pain, phantom limb, the child missing.

The child's father calls. He says they need to curtail M's visits, says they are bad for the boy. She disagrees. The child wants to see M she says mildly. In fact the child is passionate, certain, declarative. She cannot for any reasons of her own take away the child's belief that he has some little control over his own world. But when she hears herself fighting for M her stomach curdles.

She is so bad.

She is so good.

Why not give in? She is so tired after all, tired above all, an invisible weight that presses on her. Why not say yes.

You do it then.

You're in charge, you make the decision, you arrange it, you explain to our son why.

He wants to lengthen the time each parent spends with the boy. She discusses this objectively. Saying nothing of what she feels. Maybe because it's a given. Maybe it's that this longing feels weak, her need. Maybe she should get over it. Hobbies. Friends. Maybe she should get a dog finally, if it matters that much to have someone by her all the time.

Do you want to come over one night this week, she asks her child on the telephone. No, comes the small clear voice. Stay with Daddy.

She is proud of the boy, for being able to define his own desires. But the limb throbs, dragging behind her, useless, imaginary.

They have few real tempests on this part of the coast. There's an island between Vancouver and the ocean's real wrath, taking the brunt of those rolling inexorable furies. Almost nothing about her city is other than as she would wish it. But the occasional storm would be nice. Clear the air. Come, split, cascade. But no. Not for them the relief of the breaking-point, and the flood.

33.

Yesterday it turned warm, sultry even. There was a breath-lessness in the air. The first day of spring, she said, even though it was only the sixth of March. Glancing above, the sky was like porridge or curdled milk.

Life has settled into a kind of routine. A rhythm. She has an old thermos for her son's lunch. No more sandwiches to fight over, cajole and convince. She is speaking to her own parents again. M called them first. She'd been acting odd, M said. The fight, and then fleeing like that. M told them she was worried. M asked her parents to keep in touch. Instead they got in touch with her.

You don't sound crazy, her father said. Just mad as hell.

M continues to send her parents lengthy emails describing her dreams. She and M and the children in a truck, flee-ing a fire. She throws herself from the truck bed into the spooling road, ignoring their cries. M reaches for her, tries to get her to reach back. To no avail.

They forward the messages to her but she hasn't the stomach to read through to the end.

She's thrown away the baby blues and pastel pinks she wore, for a joke nobody noticed, in the far reaches of the city. Instead she lays out richer colours: a velvety eggplant dress, a close salmon-coloured raincoat, boiled red shirts and sweaters. The shirt is an ordinary snap-up crimson except for being punched all over with tiny holes. She has a frothy kind of ruffled scarlet number for wearing over another shirt, a cherry-coloured silk sash, and red shoes. Hourglass heels and a licked mauve lining, where her foot goes in. Those are some shoes, people say. She remembers to say thanks. Doesn't tell them she needs the colour, to warm her from below. Needs to be anchored, much as she can, in its shifting gleam. The banked coals, smouldering.

34.

When it rains they leave the bikes and take the bus. How much rain is the question. Gauging the rain becomes an important component of the morning. Will it stop. Will it swell into something really drenching and unpleasant. Will it clear and leave all sunny as if these leftover drops were nothing to bother about or even acknowledge. And how cold will it be, how cold will they get, will it become unbearable? When she guesses wrong a choked sob, on the half-bicycle trailing behind her, lets her know.

Mommy, it's too cold. And the child must be swathed in his mother's jacket, sleeves trailing over the trailabike handlebars, for the rest of the trip.

Before that, the paper is a clue. Her lilting voice: Can you find the weather? What does the picture say? The child is only five, he can't even read, but the mother is already asking her son to interpret the forecast. The weather report employs a number of discrete icons, from a thickly filled square of raindrops needing no interpretation to the more ambiguous "Showers," approximately half as much falling-water in the same space. There's "Mixed," sun and cloud vying for space. "Sunny" almost unheard of, coming round once a year if that.

35.

These days keeping dry is her perpetual concern. Somebody buys her child a raincoat. The child has hoods and hats, including one particularly fetching cap with fake sheepskin flaps that his father purchased for him on a snowy day. She bought her boy an expensive duffle coat that same day and they walked about like a model family, in that thickly falling forest.

The little one keeps losing gloves and hats. So does she. For Christ's sake. Not again. She goes back to the store reminding herself that two pairs of gloves in a season is reasonable where she's concerned. The new ones are made of neoprène and have a design all over them, stamped white on the grey fingers. They're designed to be dipped in water and stay warm which makes sense for her world. Looking closer she sees that each blob is a tiny spermatozoa.

Bike shops get used to her pulling the seven-foot-long contraption up to the door. She can't get it in, the child's half-bike joined to hers, there's no way. When she can't fill her own tyres an apprentice is sent to do it for her. She has to buy another light, every time she forgets to take it off it gets stolen. Three lights so far and now another one to scrape up the money for, to put on the card. She's so tired. The practicals, how they grind you down. Unreturned milk bottles, dusty floors, eventual despair. Lack of light.

36.

There comes a time when she is tired of rain. A time when she no longer welcomes or even tolerates the exciting contest between her and the elements, the one where she is determined to remain warm and dry and the rain is determined to penetrate her. Take these outer garments: fold, flap, button and zip. It's March and she is done. How tiresome the endless putting on of clothes, the endless overcovering! And more, and more, and still again more. Her tights are wearing out, holes appear in the toes. Her coats are dirty again and she's washed them once already this season.

She imagines rain, a spurned lover who won't get the hint. Imagines her voice turning harsh like with M, the times M didn't do what she wanted. Can't you see? Don't you know? She'd like to tell rain to see someone, fix its flaws. But rain can't change. Won't. And she's stuck with rain, no way of getting out of this one. Glances up at the sky, scowls. Imagines herself, free.

37.

She is angry all the time. Angry and incredulous. You'd think rain, the eternal damping of it, would temper her fire. You'd think she'd cool down. You'd imagine, she imagines, that nothing can simmer that long without burning dry and cracking, precisely, down the middle.

But she's intact, still. What go are her dishes, one at a time. Her grandmother's china has survived so much: her grandmother's lifetime and then an exciting few years with her. Barely, though. Once a man with a grudge, her son's father in fact, broke into her place and destroyed everything but the kitchenware. Staring at the stacks of dishes on the shelves, order in the midst of the carnage, she realized why. Breaking it would have made too much noise.

Fuck. Shit.

Her son has grown used to her cursing as another bowl slips clattering from her nerveless fingers. They have two left, one with a slowly blackening seam that does not bode well. Each time she reaches for it in the soapy water she says a small inarticulate prayer.

Oh. These are nice, she says to the people who bring her beautiful little tulip-shaped glasses, thick-cut teacups stamped with an unfamiliar name. She imagines the things trembling, as she holds them. Why, to the cruel god of china and glass, must this be their fate? Her faithless and inevitable hands.

It doesn't matter how careful she is. If she makes sure the stemware sits in the extreme inner part of the counter waiting its turn she breaks the glasses in the wash. Reaching out absentmindedly to put something back on the table she misses the surface entirely and over it goes. Once she broke a glass, a thick leaded tumbler, simply by banging it down on the table too hard. She isn't even always drunk, although that certainly adds to the carnage.

She carries her latest victim to the alley. Useless now, like so many other things. Outside it is raining again. Rain, what a democratic notion. Rain covers everything, even her mistakes, with a fine misting, a bumpy covering in the perpetual stand and motion of liquid. Rain is arrested, stilled in its ceaseless trajectory. Rain that bells taut against an internal suspension, wanting fruitlessly to escape itself.

She leaves rain to it. She abandons her loved and broken things to the wet.

38.

Yesterday she and the child plodded from street to street as usual, dodging puddles, dampening. Inside a steamy café she bought her child a hot milk. The woman at the next table was gruff and heavyset, ignoring them. Faintly traced moustache. Oh yes. Her child whined and wriggled and spilt the milk. She fixed him with a Look but to no avail.

Outside the rain continued, the rain in which their coast specializes. It dropped steadily onto the world, all-pervasive, impossible to ignore. She began to pretend. She imagined leaning forward and speaking to the woman, the two of them laughing. The woman would find her child adorable. Now the sun came out, the three of them would walk out together, the adults' shoulders almost touching. Later she'd get to see her naked, the stranger from the café.

On a sunny day a couple of years ago, she remembered, they sat in another coffee place like this one: she, her son, and M. She and M engaged to be married. Outside, so M the sun worshipper could take in the few rays. The child was on her lap, drinking hot chocolate. For a moment she allowed herself to picture the three of them, the fine family they made, to imagine the envy of everyone who saw them. Then the child turned and, without warning, vomited brown all over the front of her coat.

She remembers the limitless blue of the sky, that day.

39.

M kept a couple of old ponchos in the back of the Land Rover, tucked into their pouches. Probably they're there still. When rain came unexpected M would bring the jackets around to the front for them to wear.

In other respects M ignored rain as she ignored her surroundings wholesale. M had an ability, wilful it was, not to notice what was around her: stained carpet, furniture that cut into the backs of your thighs, the damp reaching in from outside. Padding barefoot onto the cold floor of the front porch on wet nights. Carrying her one giant drink. M liked drink, just not much of it; but it was in vain that she explained rum and Coke was unsuitable for cold weather.

Outside, wet licked at the stucco of the house. Lichen crawled up and around its edges. The wet window box balanced on the rail, empty but for soil, soaked it up day after day. Then the bottom gave out finally and the contents collapsed over the path. They skirted it for weeks, leaving the floorless box there, in the sky above.

40.

She listens to rain running rivulets into gutter and down-spout, rain snaking down glass and wall. Rain trickles and gushes and goes from strength to strength. This is rain's only desire, to gather and grow. Each raindrop dreams it-self a river, rushing towards the sea. Each dribble and dash swollen into an innumerable wall of its fellows. How would the sky look, full of rain? Nothing to see but water, and the city in the bottom of an aquarium with them, transfigured: swimming fish.

Rain slides off these hard smooth surfaces of concrete and glass, unable to stop or even slow its passage. The old ways were better, before man. Damp earth to dig into, wet leaves of curling fern to turn glossy in the storm. Rain making its own way. No sounds but the trickle of earth absorbing its utmost and the sudden soft collapse. The slump.

Rain as a constant condition is unknown to the ancients,

or at least invisible in the writing left us. Perhaps before rain was at least partially thwarted by our waterproofs and rubbers, nobody went out in it. Perhaps it was too banal. Perhaps you ignored rain, and this was a rule that everybody knew. A self-evident injunction, not even worth writing down.

41.

There is some shining there, where rain is, some dancing in the air. Some shimmering swaying streaks too small to fol- low. Making important things easy to ignore, as she knows to her cost. Cars, pedestrians, even lights blaring sudden yellow.

Rain dampens her shoes and curls them, and soaks the leather until it is dark with wet; and when the shoes dry, unless the glue is good, sole and upper will part in mutual disgust.

Rain brings the oil that lies in the million little holes even pavement has to the surface: planing on it, her steed's rub- ber slide towards traffic's red glow, oblivion.

Rain works its way into the crannies and nooks at the top of the house where she lived once. Rain swells there, in the dark. The smallest of plants find that moisture, like a gift, and fall to feeding. High up, inside, the wall's corner turned dark, almost ominous. They've painted it over but the mildew remains, inside, growing.

42.

Rain pulls the green from the young shoot and she rejoices to see it. Rain makes them wet & plump. Rain deadens and dances the incessant noise. Rain washes everything: people, the streets, glass. It washes down two alleys at work & home.

Rain goes down to the river. Rain goes down to the sea. Rain carves a path. Rain a funnel and conduit. Rain finding a way. Rain goes through, goes under, goes around, always ever in the same direction. Rain a constant. Rain fights and hammers. Rain is the loudest of weathers. Rain tells her to go inside. To stay there. Rain reminds her of the weight of even small things. Aide-mémoire, understanding. Rain niggles and invites and at the last mirrors.

Rain fills up the reservoirs. Rain raises the level. Rain gives her what she can take. And then some. Rain is a creek carving squiggle into the loam. A rivulet. Rain changes things. Nothing is as it was after rain.

43.

Rain today is a smattering. A muttering, a pattering on high.

Is it raining again, she says.

Sort of. Maybe.

Take the first time M grabbed her. Was it beyond the pale? Was it a sign? Could she, should she, have taken it more seriously? Should she have known that the few drops are precursors of the flood? M had a normal family after all. Normal, that strange word. Two older brothers, an idyllic childhood, so M said, on the islands, raised mostly by the soft-voiced housekeeper. You were in my way, M told her.

She said nothing. Had they done the same to her, those bigger boys, only M had never mentioned it? She would have sworn she and M had told each other everything, in those months leading up to their union. Her early hopes for the violin and odd uncle. M's past loves and their sweet, sad, inevitable partings. Nobody's fault, it seemed. Nobody to blame.

It's abuse, M screamed that day, standing in the door when someone wants to leave the room. I called the helpline and that's abuse, that and withholding the household money: you're abusing me, you're the abuser.

Surely she made some reply, surely bitter words rose in her own throat, surely she gave as good as she got?

44.

The little ferry to Granville Island moves sideways across the entrance to the creek. All kinds of vessels emerge from this mouth come summer: kayaks, big yachts, tug-tugged barges. The channel empty now, in late spring, but for hardy wetsuited rowers, harried by motorboats, their drivers shouting. She rides the ferry to fetch donuts. At water level the rain a shifting shower & curtain. The little windows of the tubby boat turning to cloud as it chugs along cheerful. Oh my hat, she murmurs.

She walks through the market and out again, carrying her brown paper bag. Smudge of grease hinting at its contents. Outside, in the grey flat sky, the rain invisible. Crossing the parking lot, wet blossom underfoot her only clue. One drop glazes her face, then another. Still looking up she sees nothing.

Later the rain turns solid and dark, hems her in. Later still she and her son ride the bus home thankful. A girl in the handicapped seats turns a face smooth as a plate towards them. Smiling, bland, ticking. Remember me?

She does, now. A teenage neighbour from the summer campsite. What has the girl heard is the question.

We're not together anymore, she says about her and M, hastily, to forestall any inquiry. But there wasn't going to be one.

I know.

And she won't let me see her and I'm mad, pipes her child. She sets her face and schools herself, saying nothing. Someone having to be the adult around here. This exercise like so many others. Don't get what you want, don't complain, don't protest, don't try to correct the record. Let the story stand.

45.

The sun is shining and it has begun to rain. But this too changes at once and in the middle of the downtown, in the city streets so built for purpose, so crowded with striding properly dressed citizens - business, all business - it begins to hail.

At first there is disbelief. Soon everyone is looking around and up as the little orbs bounce on the ground. The tourists are amazed. Hail is the word in every mind, on every lip. Some let it escape despite the universal prohibition on speaking aloud. The hail too extraordinary for normal precautions. The women hold out their hands supplicating, palms to the sky. Their little shoes and hose no protection against rain turned sudden hard. Rolling pebbles gathering white in the gutters.

Under her feet now stars burst, each small ball spread and caught against grey concrete, an intricate expanding pattern of splayed ice. Footprints outlined against the flattened hail underfoot. Preserved but the permanence is illusory. A degree or two rise and hail will vanish as if it never existed. Only those out in this imperfect hour, eleven o'clock, too late for coffee too early for lunch, will be able to attest. A whole morning might pass before anyone inside thinks to glance through their windows, to observe the outside world. Nonsense, they'll say. It's just rain. Looks perfectly ordinary to me.

46.

On weekends it rains. In the morning mother and child rise no later than usual but in no hurry, that's the great thing. Saturdays miss the paper, stay in bed. At leisure clear the tea things, tray and pitcher and little pot. Up crank the oven, match to flame: a small enamelled oblong, white with stains of half-century. Modern Maid.

She bakes. Cornbread, banana bread, puffed yellow German pancake. Something hot to table. Inside they sit ignoring the streaming gloomy world. Lifting cakes still warm to their mouths, buttering the crumbly slices with voluptuous concentration. Their world shrunk to yellow box, small and warm and most importantly dry.

47.

For days weather has toyed with them. A few drops here and there, heralds, and then above, the innocent blank sky. Promising permanence.

But she knows otherwise. That the sun showing like a disc of mirror through a cloudy scrim is illusory. That rain always comes back.

Standing in the park where the dogs run and run or worry at bones, their flanks splashed and rubbed with the mud of the field. The rain has wet the earth that comes up amongst the too-thin grass. The dog owners are out in all weathers, perfectly comfortable, they are used to it and stand astride as in their own hallways. She stands, too, looking after the dogs in their curious pack-like symmetry. In this position the whole of the sky is open to her. She can see weather coming. Closer to the water, at the end of the street, the clouds break and wander off. The lowering sun ducks under their edge in curiosity, its pale red-gold glow irradiating the silvery edge of the water.

48.

Suddenly August. Sun swims up to every day's allotted square, turning the forecast into a repeat. The people have waited so long. In Vancouver sun is a kind of fruit, seasonal. Everyone has the same urge, to gorge. To go down to the sun. To bask in it. To forget there is such a thing as rain. Collective amnesiacs who stare each autumn in unfeigned dismay, faces blank. What, this again? It's raining? Forgetting as an act of self-preservation. Nonsense, they say. It doesn't rain like that. It can't. There's no way. A hundred days of rain one after the other? Certainly not. And the thing is, nobody lies, not consciously.

She knows she and her son need to soak up enough sun to see them through, it's a physical necessity. She insists they visit the beach every night after work, after she fetches the child from camp. The days are long, there's plenty of time.

We'll have fish and chips again. These can be sublime, or

greasy and soaked, depending on the teenager wielding the fryer. They aren't always the sharpest, these concession-aires. She asked one to heat up a baby bottle for her once and the girl obligingly unscrewed the top and started run-ning hot water into the milk.

Yay, fish and chips. It doesn't cross her child's mind to resent her attempts at bribery. Or they take picnics. She wraps up fried things in bread, wraps those in turn in brown paper fastened with elastic bands. Leftover squares of wax paper if she can get them, if she's bought meat at the deli this week. What a luxury, forgetting it rains.

49.

Now you, he says. It's the first and last month of summer. They've come for the day: she, her son's father, her son, a neighbour to take her son on the Ferris wheel and pirate ship. The mother and son have already done all the rides the mother will go on without balking: the Tilt-A-Whirl, the bumper cars, the Scrambler. Rides that stick close to the ground.

No.

Come on.

I don't want to.

You're going to.

She looks up at the rickety wooden structure of the roller coaster, listens to the clack-clack of the cars going up.

Screams from the far side, the drop. That lurch in her stomach as they stand in line. It's a long lineup she tells herself but it seems only moments before they're at the front.

Get in.

I don't want to.

She finds herself on the small bench seat. He crowds in beside her. They go up. Then the poised instant, in the sky. She screams as they fall, as she knew she would, as you do in nightmares, and as in nightmares the wind catches the scream from her.

That wasn't so bad, was it?

No. Staggering out, her knees knocking.

Let's go again.

Okay, she says, despite herself.

50.

Across town, on the side of the hill overlooking the river, her old house. M in it still, barefoot, padding. Rain pattering on the porch, collecting in pools, the wood they needed to do something about. In the corner of the wall, under the eaves, if you knew where to look, the plaster worn away, exposing the lath. In the far yard, morning glory mounding the fence. Its trumpet flowers turned up to the sky triumphant.

In the house the bedroom window gives onto a vista, the ground sloping steeply away underneath. Their neighbours' houses like toys. The screams from the amusement park across the river wafted towards them caught and swirling away, as the roller coaster whips its passengers around.

Below their hill are the docks. Lights of industry twinkling, empty sidings from where trains once slid to a stop, to be filled or disgorged. The large and mysterious arrangement of buildings without windows or discernable purpose, their lots floodlit, overlooking the water.

Clouds drift across the face of deep indigo hills on the adjacent shore. In her time she could imagine it raining there, on the other side, as she and M watched the water from their bedroom window. From this far above, the river is planed jade, calm as a just-made bed.

She had the carpets torn up. Floors refinished. Kitchen painted. M did her part. M had a woman in to paint the guest room.

Finish it, M told the woman.

The primer hasn't had a chance to dry yet, the painter said, pointing to the corner. You paint it now, the mould will just come through again.

I don't care. We can't wait any longer for the office. Within the week the dark bloom back, as the painter predicted, under the new colour: a shadow, an uneasiness in the corner of an eye.

What about a dormer window upstairs. What about making the front porch bigger.

She brought home four chairs, a table. They ate overlooking the water. No use. The familiar thickness in the air, broken only by complaint.

What's this stuff.

I can't eat it, it's too spicy.

Everyone but her pushing back their plates.

Later, M heated mac and cheese in the microwave, in the kitchen at night.

Unhappiness seemed so futile then and the people that suc-cumbed unimaginative. Leaving was a fool's answer, too final by half, like suicide. I don't see why people break up, she'd say. Surely they could do something else, take a trip, move, go back to school. She waited for M to agree.

She read more self-help books. Should You Leave, and the answer, as she already suspected, always No.

Then the last day, although she didn't know it then, had no suspicion this was any different from any other fight except worse.

Then the police pulling up, putting an end to half measures.

51.

Lies come sliding into her office on thin sheets, stamped with the name of a prominent firm of attorneys. It becomes imperative to find her own lawyer, to construct her own misconstructions, to keep up with the Ms.

At the case conference she leaned over and asked M. Why are you doing this?

Stop talking to me.

Why are you bothering? You'll just have to spend a ton of money and it'll all go to lawyers anyway.

Stop it. I said stop it.

Then she got it. She felt stupid for not having grasped the point earlier. The spending of the money on the lawyers, making sure that none of it reached her.

The curling paper accuses her of not declaring her assets. She owns, it says, an expensive road bike. A motorcycle. An expensive bike trailer. The list makes her smile.

Today the rain is back, adding its sibilance to the chorus of traffic. Antiphony, counterpoint. Cars swish in the new wet. The window has been open all night. Her dwarf conifers in a line outside the two windows are brave little soldiers: she hasn't had to water them once this year. One of them grows slightly crooked, which could be said of the best of them.

They're still alive, she told friends at dinner. I don't know what to do.

You'll have to uproot them, her boss said. Container gardening is a brutal business.

52.

It rained on her and M's first anniversary, she remembers. They checked into the venerable island resort where M's parents stayed the first night of their marriage. They would come back every year, she and M told each other.

The hotel was on the seafront and everything through the windows was bluey grey: sea, sand, sky. They lay in bed, a year on, the windows open. Conversations from the beach walk below came in as if the people were right outside the room.

In the morning the motorcycle wouldn't start.

Ah man.

The motorcycle was an old one. It had been her wedding present to M who said she wanted one. M had trouble with the starter, though, and never drove it. She wouldn't have cared except that in the meantime she'd fallen in love. An accident. Her first drive on the bike was to the garage where she'd found a place to store it until the big day. Another rainy afternoon off the ferry, wet whispering of tyres on the highway.

She should have been terrified at the ancient engine, the mechanical know-how its age and British engineering, if you could call it that, demanded. But the motorcycle got into her blood instead, and this despite all the times she stood by to watch it be hauled off by yet another tow truck. A profane affair, cyclist run reeking up to the pumps. Shameful and exciting. As she urged the slow engine up the long hill on the way to the ferry the rest of the traffic ran past.

It was always an adventure seeing if the thing would start. Sometimes she forgot and treated it like an ordinary motorcycle, pulled up to the front, driving outfit on, first warm day of the year. She put on the helmet and settled herself astride. Then she stomped on the starter. There was a fatal click and nothing else.

Oh yeah. That's right.

Sometimes it was a little thing they could put right in a moment, sometimes it meant another sojourn at the garage. The morning of their anniversary she and M stood around and waited while the tow truck came. It'd be ready to run again that same day, the driver told them. Nothing but a tripped switch or crossed wire, a battery gone down. See, she said, that wasn't so bad.

Let's just get home, M said. Their anniversary was over.

53.

She looks out another highrise office window, past another lawyer at another wide desk. Below, the city spreads itself, the normally hidden rooftops slowly darkening with moisture. Today the report came true. One hundred percent chance of precipitation.

The lawyer begins to describe the advantages of divorce. She interrupts.

It's not about that, she says. It's about keeping my vow. I made a promise.

Who keeps their vow arguing, moving out, battling over furniture? One thing she can cling to. She never asked for a divorce. She stayed with M, well, maybe not with M exactly, maybe miles off, in the same city, but the idea remains, they're tied, somehow.

So it doesn't make sense. Why one thing and not the other? To make herself feel better. To salve her burning conscience.

What does she have to feel guilty about?

Not being able to endure.

54.

M who is still her spouse phones her. She glances out the window at the fallen night. Wet as usual. She remembers that her bicycle is still out in the drip, has been out since the afternoon in fact, and will stay there overnight, contrary to her rule. Tomorrow morning at the latest she must collect it.

After the first flat, two days ago, she patiently transferred her steed from bus to bus, five in all, to the repair shop and then home. Her son patient too, accompanying her. One of the drivers lectured her that the bus she was on, despite its rack, should not accept her bicycle: the route was not designated for them. He would let her on, this once. She forebore to argue, unusual for her. Her arm still aches from lifting that weight to the height of the bus racks, over and over, and muscling it into place.

Yesterday, as she rode through the same intersection, another thunk and report. She ignored the obvious conclusion until it was forced upon her, the rubber pancaked against the pavement. She remembered then that this is the way flat tyres come: none for months, anything up to a year, and then a cluster of them. She rolled the once again suddenly useless machine to the nearest post and affixed it.

I'm late again, she said on the phone to the school. She was at the same corner, calling from the same endangered public phone.

Afterwards she got on the bus. A young woman embarked at the next stop. The young woman didn't have all of the money for the fare and said so plainly and nicely. The driver ordered her off. Too late she realized she could have paid the extra for the girl. Should have. Too late, as the bus pulled away from the stop. Patient girl, and she failed her.

Later, after she has dried out and changed, eaten until her stomach is a drum, and put the child to bed, M calls. M wants to know, though she doesn't say so, why her visits with the child are suddenly curtailed. The answer, what she won't say in reply to M's unspoken question, is that her child's father persuaded her to it, against her own better judgment. Her son's grief for artifact.

I called him but he never called back, M says instead. What exactly is happening tomorrow?

Call him.

He didn't call me back.

M asks to talk to her son. She says the child is asleep.

I don't believe you.

It happens to be true. She laughs and says goodbye and hangs up on another one of M's threats.

55.

This morning rain goes from scattered drops to downpour in a seeming matter of moments. The mechanic glances outside the windows of the bike shop where he bends over the slowly revolving wheel.

Another lovely day.

I'd still rather be biking, she says, thinking of her adventures on the bus yesterday, and the day before that.

Wheeling her fixed machine out of the shop, she hunches ineffectively against rain going about its work. The noise of rain, the not-noise really, blots out anything else. A rushing, a pushing, a surround. The world through a screen, a fine mesh. Even traffic exists far behind it, an afterthought. Soon enough the rain becomes aggregate. The individual drops melt together and hang on her, their weight palpable. Soon after that rain takes over entirely. A mass of rain, a mob of it. Soon afterwards she gives up. Nothing happens, only she knows she's drenched and accepts it, as it's said you eventually accept death.

A leap of rain. A plummet of it.

A suicide of rain, falling.

56.

They were still living together. M never liked to be called her wife.

I'm your spouse.

Trying to humour M was tiring, especially when there was no return on it. Eventually she gave up.

They were arguing in a hotel room on their annual trip to the resort. M had promised to give up the rum and Coke. She'd come back to the used glass, the discarded tin. So obvious. She'd been in the bowels of the building, reading the historical plaques. She found the pint in M's suitcase.

That's mine, M cried. Her child watched as they sawed back and forth.

Not in front of the child.

Give it back.

She took the boy and left the room. M followed her, jumping up into her face. Outside rain smattered them both. She took the steps turned dark down to the gritty beach under the hotel. Instinct, going to the sea which had always soothed her. The shore coloured slate, sky and water both, private docks and boats in the cove with that deserted wintry look. Nobody was coming back for them for quite some time if ever. The wood under her feet felt slick with the rain that lay on the boards where they were hollowed out by clanking landlubber feet, the boards themselves swollen with moisture. She knew this weather inside out, it ran in her veins. The interminable view of fat splattered drops and sullen indifferent sky.

M bobbed in front of her, trying to get a rise. I'm going to follow you around the beach the whole way. I'll follow you all day. How do you like that? Huh? Huh?

It's okay, she said. I'm always trying to get you to take walks with me.

M turned abruptly and went back to the glassed-in lounge.

There were a lot of arguments and most of them not even that cute. Why couldn't they fix things anyway? Ah that was the question. The psychiatrist was avuncular, he sat back in his big chair and gave advice. The therapist who phoned her afterwards concerned. Another one told them they were in the conflict stage. You don't say. Once they got a man at the plumbing store to arbitrate. It worked as well as anything else.

57.

A radio outside her building, invisible around the corner, squawks to faraway life. Question and report. A fine rain stipples the outside of the screens.

In the afternoon rain begins in earnest. Soon rain comes billowing out of the sky, a celestial housewife shaking her sheets. What light there was fades to dark but the dark is not complete. Caught in it dancing are these gusts and eddies, the innumerable drops highlighted by street lamps.

Going down the short slope of Thurlow Street on the way to the station to pick up S she sees water running over the pavement. It cascades in serried ranks, a series of broad rounded scales descending in swift and stately fashion towards lower ground. A couple passes her, a lady of a certain age, a man wearing a homburg under his giant black umbrella. The woman smiles as they cross. Figures from another era. These days nobody would walk in such conditions, not unless they had to.

She goes to the station to wait for S's bus. It's an hour late as a rule. All these back and forths, the sheer numbing weight of them. Time. The constancy. How this partial and unspoken connection has become her mainstay, a thin thread connecting their separate cities. Her lover's shoulders bowed, the legacy of a father absent at the time and since vanished entirely. Slender enough, for the weight of both of their various failures. Marriage being only her most visible, the sign. Neither of them talk to their relations: they exist in peculiar fashion, the issue of springs or tree branches, as in the myths.

The next day it is still raining. She and S walk across the art deco bridge, with its towers in the middle. There are viewing platforms built into the skirts of the towers, there are steps up from the ground beneath as the bridge rises from the side of the hill. As always she measures the distance to the water with her eyes: toy boats beneath, the bay a misty bowl seeded over by rain's fierce attentions, the pocked surface churned in its depths. How easy it would be, she thinks as ever, to balance there, with the water's promise beneath. To vault over or step off. Just do it.

As always she keeps these thoughts to herself.

As pedestrians she and S are soon enough undone. Her hat turned sodden, S's stained ball cap dripping, their same-sex boots wicking up the splash in mahogany profusion. Their coats heavy on their backs. Where her shoulders stick up into the air she can feel a thin line of wet running across the top of her shirt. Weather getting in.

In the movie theatre they're just in time for the feature. They hang their outerwear on adjacent seats with a fine sense of futility. The movie takes place in a misty warm country. The heroine wears a lot of filmy dresses. Her body heavy and delicious, like fruit. How old is the ripe young actress? Twenty-two? She has read the number in a gossip magazine but it's like so much else, slipped past, submerged.

When they pick their coats up afterwards, shuffle back to the lobby as the credits roll, their suspicions are confirmed. The coats have if anything become wetter, the soak settling in. They walk glumly to the noodle house with its bench seats. Jostling boys at the next table.

My dad's going to give me the UBC apartment if I go to UBC, she hears one of them say. These are West Side kids, she thinks, thinking also that nobody she knows would utter such a sentence, ever.

Their coats are still heavy. Defeated, they queue for the bus and ride across the bridge. Wet and steamy there, inside, but at least warm. The rain continues. The whole of S's visit, in fact, it never stops.

58.

Three trips in the wet black, wearing her flower-pot hat as she dashes into cars, into stores. The design on the back of her plain dark coat picked out in reflective tape. The irregular starburst she applied herself lies dully against the black fabric until, catching the light briefly, it flares into sudden brightness.

I thought a bull's eye would be too obvious, she tells anyone who asks.

Her pal Trouble parks, walks, orders harshly, lifts the café cup trembling to her lips. Trouble has problems as always. She has scant time for Trouble, still more than anyone else from what Trouble tells her. Something foamy in the depths of the cup, a smear across Trouble's upper lip.

Later that night, having seen Trouble off, she waits for a ride from Nurse. They are still dating, in curious suspended fashion. Curious only to her maybe. She has lost her faith, if she ever had it. Imagining that she could understand anyone else, what they're thinking or will do next. Just as dangerous, throwing up her hands in this way, as she has reason to know, but the alternative not to be contemplated, the dark nights without even a television for company.

Hours ago the dark descended, or rather the orange-tinted not-dark that the city offers. Down the lanes red tail lights explode sudden flowers. Nurse slides the big vehicle from street to street like a dealer handling cards.

They come to rest, engine off: Nurse leaves her. Immediately she is surrounded by the sound of rain. The vehicle a blind for the hunting of rain. Pattering, smattering, tinkling, trickling. Pale rain shadows puddle overhead, on the arching glass. They gather and streak across, shadowing the broad plastic expanse of the dash with their trails. As soon as seen, gone again. As if protesting this, rain kicks. It tickles the roof, pounds miniscule fists, drums tiny heels on the body of the car. Streaming, rain drops at last, its weight insupportable. In the back, the bicycles steam. Her coat emits its fetid smell of damp.

The next morning, a message from her lawyer. M, surprise, has been calling the lawyer, demanding replies: each response to cost hundreds of dollars, as she knows from experience. The lawyer is too smart for M though. She doesn't respond and then reports. This is what happened. Let me know if your instructions change. If only everyone would act like this, do exactly as she tells them.

59.

On the weekdays, scanty showers, driblets, interspersed with peekaboo sun or sullen cloud. On the weekends, rain, sudden and torrential. All-encompassing. Week after week and month after month this pattern continues.

It's easy, someone says. There's all this traffic. Monday to Friday. Then it stops.

The explanation can't be right but the pattern imposes its own truth, or logic. Saturday comes, a torrent. Water pouring between buildings, the hollow drowning fall of it. In the morning she lies in bed listening to rain. It's early, there are no noises to get in the way. The very occasional swish of a car pursuing its blind blunt way down the hidden street outside, at the front. The water a cascade, a cavalcade, a call to arms, a march. It depresses one, the very regularity of it. The inevitability. You will get wet again. Yes you will, no matter if you buy cute rubbers and a bright mackintosh. No matter where you store your umbrella. Despite the magazines that exhort you to this new colour or kicky print. Dots.

Lying there she imagines that the deluge comes from somewhere closer than cloud, a discarded hose pouring. Loosed hydrant in the sky. The little trees on the windowsill skewed. Cascade on the glass. Rain continues inevitable.

60.

November. She attends a criminal trial where her fate is to be decided. The accused. She wears the same clothes she wore on the day she apparently viciously assaulted M: the skirt, the little sweater, the wedge heels. Even the pearls.

Do you accept. Has it been proven that. Two days of this, increasingly removed. The details of this trial are sealed, their publication banned. In vain she argues against this.

Her son's father attends both days. He slouches in the visitor's gallery wearing an uncouth T-shirt. At the recess he walks her to lunch. Outside it is always raining, lightly, but she doesn't feel a thing on her as they pass over the brick streets with their allotment of grey. They end up in a warm cloudy restaurant, full of people whose innocence is not in doubt. Try to eat, he says.

Back to the judge, who says simply: I don't know who to

believe. She is acquitted on all counts. I frankly do not think this belonged in a courtroom, the judge says.

I am sure she believes what she says is true, he says of M, kindly.

M stands up after the verdict, all five foot three of her quivering. The small head lifts in an invisible wind. Bullies always win, she says bitterly.

Unusually a riposte comes to her at once. Not this time, she replies, before the bailiffs crowd in.

61.

Saturday again, raining again. Looking out the window at the sliver of air between her and the next building she sees no space into which her body, the size of a human being, might insert itself. The wet presses down so unrelentingly that she turns to her son.

Let's just leave.

And the child, all of six, replies at once: Okay.

They take the elevated railway to the bus station. The bus for Victoria has gone, another will not come for hours. Outside again, the rain unchanged, they dash for the el station where she has left the transfers for anyone who needs them. Nobody has. They are still there on the floor, only slightly damped.

They get on a bus in the rain. They get off. They get on another bus in the rain. They get off. They get on another bus in the rain. They get off. They get on the last bus, the one that will take them to the ferry. Movement, she's decided, is what she needs, that and some distance from the piles of paperwork she should be doing. In her pack are a couple of pieces of paper, a pen, but no matter how long she sits and where she goes she knows she won't even uncap the lid.

The next ferry to Victoria won't leave for an hour and a half. The cashier glares at the man in front of them as they idle in his wake. He is buying a ticket for the boat to Nanaimo. She tells him he has ten minutes.

You're lucky you're getting on, says the cashier sourly. Behind them, outside, the rain is a soft, unrelenting murmur on the concrete apron of the drop-off area. The automatic doors whisk open and shut. Drops linger in their hair and speckle their bags. It's the last ferry of the night, continues the clerk.

Two to Nanaimo, she says.

The cashier tries to glare at them too, but has used most of it up on the man in front. I'm busy, she says instead, when asked about buses into Nanaimo. I don't have time. But she has time to give them instructions, extremely detailed ones, about how to get to the ferry's car deck.

They run through the rain for the open maw of the boat. Her son is game, his superhero knapsack bouncing behind him as he trots with great concentration. The workers await them on the ramp, their pickup truck drawn up with lights flashing. Inside, the echoing hold is stained with the wet tracks of their predecessors. The ferry workers direct them up the stairs with a fine offhand concern, one that feels almost like love. The kind she wants, not the kind she can get.

62.

In the morning in the unfamiliar room (three beds, no table, no chair) the mist is a low-lying thing on the rooftops. Gathered rain and leaves lie in the hollow of the flat roofs.

You come to Nanaimo to get away from rain? snorts the woman in the polyester housecoat, the one who lives here for the winter. She has waffles and syrup for breakfast, taking up the last of the sweet with her spoon. Good luck.

She is a know-it-all, this woman. She is disappointed that they are locals; otherwise she could give them advice.

There's a great train trip, she turns to the two girls with accents. You go up to Prince Rupert. Across to Jasper.

You can't do everything, one of the girls murmurs, before they shoulder their giant packs. They take everything with them, like extra bodies they must heft from place to place.

Once she too took that long trek to a faraway continent and for some reason it was equally important that she bring as much as she could carry and more. But why? Surely when you are going here and there only a couple of outfits suffice, nobody's going to see you long enough to notice, for one thing. But how fragmentary and partial it seemed, that heavy bag of hers! She had not yet learned how little she needed really. She hadn't even gotten rid of her parents.

The best laid plans of underpackers are felled by rain. You need a couple of heavy outfits, one to dry while you wear the other, especially if the rain continues. One summer biking in Europe she took one of those instant raincoats, the kind packed into a baggie. It didn't rain once that trip and she was grateful. So she didn't use the coat until she was on a ride up to Lion's Bay with some insanely chipper members of the local bike club. She stayed behind in the corner store, drinking coffee, while they went up a mountain just for the fun of it and came back.

To her mind the route they took to the village and home was a joke, a cruel one. The road undulated, a picture-book snake. Up the hill. Down the hill. Up the next hill. She imagined planners chortling as they decreed: put up the signs here, tell cyclists they are welcome. If they survive.

The familiar drops began to stipple her in warning on the return. She stopped at the top of the hill, and unfolded her raincoat. She was pleased with her foresight. The plastic was much thinner than she had expected, its area enormous. She arranged the thing over her clothes as best she could and set off. As she gathered speed a flapping, crackling noise grew around her. It was the giant garbage bag of the raincoat, catching wind like a sail.

63.

Her son away tonight, rain holds off. In the clouds as she leaves work, though, a muttered threat. Rain tonight puts her in mind of toughs who pass a bit too close in the school hallway, bump you sort-of accidentally into the lockers. The cool and clang of it. Go ahead, complain. Come on, report us. The menace of rain, impending.

She chains up, walks quickly through the whooshing automatic doors of the store. Dinner to get. Something to eat. Her head bowed, face averted: no-see-um.

Out on the street again, the rain takes its first tentative shoves, tries its weight, like a bully dancing on tiptoe. Water, skycut, jabs unprotected faces & necks and as quickly retreats. She picks up her steps, hurries a little faster along the ugly street of shops. Almost done now, almost time to turn towards home.

Inside her own door at last, barricaded behind stone and brick, she is brave enough to face rain foursquare. Curled lip. Ostentatious flick of sleeve: see, dry.

Imagines herself, good as untouched.

64.

Today rain falls faster than ever, as if human hurry is catching. Rain a sudden model of efficiency. The consultants came some time ago. They crowd the clouds, measuring drops per square inch. They catch and weigh individual drops, calculate area saturated by length of time. They have reports to make, procedures to recommend. Good news. With proper use of technology, they declare in triumph, rain can be made to fall that much faster.

It's true rain has never been exactly, how you say, career weather. Drifting and dropping, that's pretty much the extent of rain's job description. If rain had a resumé it would be a little puffy thing, a breath of wet air that disappeared when someone opened the envelope. Someone in a little room in a little office into which no rain is allowed, ever.

This is the way of the new world and rain can't fall behind. Hurry up, faster. Check your phone. Text someone. Check the website, get directions, grab another coffee (large, larger, largest: you decide), check your email, check your texts. Text someone else. Go over here, go over there, send another email, try to set up a meeting, try again, try one more time, give up. No! Giving up isn't allowed.

In the office they are packing boxes. Outside rain falls on the alley, muffling in its effect. The phone rings: it's M. Now that the criminal aspect has been decided, M can call anytime. And does. M wants to discuss some detail of the child's rota of pickups and drop-offs. Some question M's decided needs clarification.

I'll tell you if there's a change in the schedule. Goodbye, she says, and hangs up before M can reply.

Are you so desperate to talk to me, she wishes she'd said, to make up all these excuses to call? So many things M could do, to start making amends for her monstrous wrongs. Set the record straight. Admit her culpability. Calling her at work nowhere on the list. Why infuriate her needlessly when she is the one ensuring M's visits, ensuring the child has time with M - she who honours the child's wishes, to a point at least? Oh how noble. Please.

She thrills at the prospect of speaking her mind to M, even in fancy. But mostly she's astounded at herself. How is it, this far from their abrupt division, that M's voice still moves her to trembling fury? That she loses her powers of speech in rage?

Rain can be all these different things, she tells her co-worker Romany.

Nah, says Romany. Rain is rain.

65.

Surprise. A process server lurks outside the door to the alleyway. Rage & violation. Another set of documents. Requisition, affidavit, writ of summons, notice of motion: she hardly knows, and reading won't enlighten her, experience has taught, only panic. Something to do with her separation, with the child's visits, no doubt. Her finances yet again, a few pieces of paper discovered missing in the reams she's passed over. Why the bundle has to be given to her this way, like a drug or a secret, cash in a sack, another legal mystery.

But she takes the papers as she's supposed to, shoves them in her bag for later, when her chest will slow its twitter and thrum. Time enough to read them, then, and puzzle out what they are telling her. Such a nice man, the process server, for someone nobody ever wants to see.

The rain continues. All day there is a solid wall of it wherever she turns, rain hemming her in. Too wet to bike. Too wet to do anything but try and stay out of it, behind the windows of the bus.

The thin man who lives next door to her son's father gets on the bus. He embraces her as she's reading the papers. M's requesting more time with her son, this time confirmed by the court. M proposes a complicated schedule which, as she reads it, reveals itself as an increase in the time M will have with him. M's suggesting a report by a qualified psychologist who will spend time with them all and interview the child. Who will make a recommendation regarding custody and access. She remembers how she and M fought fiercely against the possibility of this same report, in court, when her son's father wanted one. How bitterly M railed against the possibility of intrusion.

Everything will work out, the thin man says. You're the mom.

If only everyone understood this. If only she could be so sure. Break the surface for a moment, rise above the undertow. Instructions she wants to give. Her own: trust self. Trust things to work out. To M: give it up. Give thanks for what you've got. Stop bothering me.

66.

Finally even she begins to talk about weather.

This rain is killing me, she says.

Four of them are sitting at a long table with a view of the
harbour. Outside the port glows with harsh orange light
and outsize painted machinery. Humming helicopters
skim angular towards the heliport. Cutting rain into mist.
Below, where she can't see unless she walks to the window
itself, boxcars painted brown & orange clash on rows of
rusty tracks. Everyone nods at her words.

How are you, she asks the woman at the tea store. They
talked so nicely last time she came.

Fine, the clerk lets out, clipped. Her face grim.

She leans forward and confides: This weather is driving me crazy.

The clerk nods.

How are you handling it, she asks the waiter at a restaurant later. She has these secret intelligent conversations with her servers these days. Co-conspirators. She's one of them or they're like her. Hard to tell.

Last year was the worst, he allows in turn. My first winter here.

But last winter it didn't rain as much as it's raining now, she counters. Arguing though there's nothing to argue about. Neither of them having to turn to the window behind her table, so sure are they already of what's to see: the streaming damp, the fast-walking pedestrians, their collars turned up and faces averted from rain's punishment.

I don't know, he answers. Seems like it rained pretty much every day then, too.

That's when she remembers the woman's reply, as she hands back the change: I think it's driving everyone crazy.

67.

Today at last a gift of clear sky. Sunshine even, she thinks peering upwards. Quick, let's get out there into the world and soak it up. My God they are pale plants. Look at her in particular: weedy & thinned, like something reared in darkness. Her limbs clotted milk.

Too late. The sun gone that sudden, disappeared behind another cloudy curtain. And now she begins to track its oscillation, here and vanished, the sun a veiled dancer on the sky's wide stage. Sun is the star of the show, the one everyone's come to see, but the sightlines in this cabaret are too bad. Sun is visible only behind a shoulder, over a bald head, one bare ray excitingly cocked. Then that disembodied limb withdraws and again she has to guess at what sun is doing.

Let's pretend. Ignore this wind-ridden edge of damp. Imagine a world of sun. What kind of people would they be, if they didn't have rain to contend with? Would they grow expansive under the warmth? Would their natures become sweet and pliable, softened by the sun? She tries to remember warm people. How boring it was, in California: day after day of blue. How tediously predictable. How they stood it. The people bland too, smiling, smoothed.

I hate it here, says the woman who cuts her hair. The people here are shit. The other day I fell full-length in the crosswalk and nobody even stopped to see if I was okay. I was dressed nice too. The car that had to drive around me didn't even roll down his window to ask if I was all right. I made eye contact with this one woman and she went Humph. People are awful. I started to cry because nobody helped me. My umbrella got all broken when I fell on it.

68.

Sun again today. In the forecast more sun for the first time she can remember since they slid back into the primordial ooze weeks or months or years ago. Oh please let it be spring, not the tease of a day or two clear and then the relentless sock of weather's worst. On Friday's square, though, clouds mass.

Going round to see lawyers who are too busy to see her. Too busy herself. Crafting affidavits in response:

No.

No.

No.

That's not how I remember it.

That's not true.

And finally, stiffly: the Plaintiff exaggerates her role.

After all the child has a mother and father already. How much he can continue to be divided, the question.

69.

Across the sky, above them, complaints of seagulls. Mommy, said her son, the first morning they woke in this apartment, on this street. I can hear the roosters howling. It was the gulls calling, far above them.

On the way to the bar a single songbird trills in a tree at the corner of Adanac and Main. Querulous, confident, the bird repeats its song. As often as necessary. The cherry blossoms are out. The SkyTrain station down the street is awash with them, on the pavement above the stairs leading down to the platform. She walks underneath gazing up in a kind of wonder. There's no profit in this profusion, no private enterprise. The blossoms are waxy and thickly clustered, their colour the lightest, most bare blush of pink. The petals drift down a different sort of rain, a kinder one.

70.

Cloudy sky again today. The panes of glass on the angled roof opposite opaque with that featureless white nobody could love. The clouds have socked them in, leaving few clues to what will come. The season is changing but here at the edge it's impossible, really, to see what shape it will be. Whether rain will move away for good and, if it does, what exactly will take its place.

In midafternoon it is sunny contrary to the forecast. A stiff wind worries the world. By evening as she and the boy hurry out to dinner the first drops have begun to fall. Portents, they warn her of what will coming. What she can expect. Nightfall comes late, at least according to her usual timetable. Winter is ebbing and she must adjust just as she adjusted to the creeping dark, the fading light. Just as the year was nibbled away to a thin grey sliver it now turns back towards her shimmering.

Saturday cleaning. The child is caught by the excitement of washing walls, wiping mirrors: he swipes barely with a rag, wanders to the next spot. Surfaces, and their potential transformation. A scrim of cloud drifts across the morning sky: promises, portent, imagine.

71.

In the daytime the sky is cloudy with rubbed-away parts like a slowly tarnishing piece of silver. Rain holding off for now. As the blue deepens into dark a pale circlet of moon comes up low on the horizon. A ghost or exposure of planet riding there at the threshold of consciousness.

She returns to the bicycle rack outside the station late at night to pick up her machine. What are you doing there, she says to the man who starts up. He has been standing, leaning over the rack. Not waiting to see his bolt cutters or lock pick, his bad bicycle intentions. Assuming his guilt quicker for them both.

Get away from my bike.

Loud protests. I was just sitting here, etc.

Her reproaches mechanical, without heat. You ought to be

ashamed. And unshackling her bicycle - her decent, law-abiding bicycle - she wheels it away.

72.

Last night S came to town. They went home together as always. S's body so known to her she could trace its outline in the dark. Their rehearsed sleeping. S's night sweats and insomnia. Her morning litany. I was up for hours last night, S will say, while you slept. I heard the sirens going by on the way to the hospital. Rarely she wakes and it's true: S, lying on her back, eyes open.

This morning S has a new report: it rained last night. Then again, a question: Did it rain last night?

Outside, blue sky. So it wasn't real: a dream, an apparition, S's imagination. And then the clue: a few drops clinging still, to the glass opposite.

She reads about her neighbourhood in the newspaper she fetches from the mat in front of her door. Sitting up in bed with tea in a thin china cup. S's coffee in a gleaming silver mug. Their routine of displacement, one or the other not at home, visiting always. According to the organizer of "Save St. Joe's," the old Catholic hospital nearby will move. His group wants it to stay in the neighborhood. The public consultation, he says, will be a sham. The only part of the hospital that will stay on the current site is the brick main building, which will provide services to addicts.

Nonsense, says the hospital spokesperson in the same article. This is his counsel, if people would only listen. His high-powered advice. The lesson he would like everyone to learn: what you can't see, isn't happening.

73.

Her child's father is in love with somebody else.

Are you seeing anybody, she asks him on the phone. At the other end, through the uniformly bad connection, the crackle like poor weather, she hears him caper and dance. He flips and rolls and whoops and finally comes to a sort of stop. Yeah.

Are you in love with her. Again the show. Now she can hear instruments, a tambourine, bells on a strap, electric mandolin. She waits, schooling herself to a patience she doesn't feel.

Why would you ask me that, he asks, the shimmy & tinkle slowing finally to silence.

Our son said you were.

155

Whooping, weaving, ducking, he goes off into peals of theatrical laughter. She's already bored in her unwilling role of audience, it's a thankless one. She'd like to do a little performing of her own: yawn audibly, crack her knuckles, hold a conversation with someone else while still on the phone. Laugh at something on TV, except she doesn't have one. But of course she doesn't.

Yeah, he says finally, thoughtfully, as if it's just occurred to him himself. I guess I am.

74.

She is disappointed in weather. She thought that when rain ended her troubles would be over. But the clear sky brings her more bitter cold than she thinks she has a right to expect. Walking in the alley in the crisp morning air, sharp as a just-bitten apple, she measures the circumference of the big jots of rain that sit like cushions on car roofs. They've driven in that morning, from Abbotsford or the Townships, with their cargo of weather. Two blocks away is the photocopy shop next to the court, where the clerk helps her make three copies of her latest affidavit: denunciations, denials, I verily believe it to be true. Her response incomplete & mistaken, no doubt, as usual. She'll take the copies to the court registry, be told by a barely civil clerk that they won't do, maybe be told what to do to make them right. Maybe. The clerks aren't supposed to help her: it falls under the category of legal advice. Mercy's opposite. She already knows she's a fool at this kind of thing, she doesn't need to be told again, but there's no choice in the matter.

It was hailing at three o'clock last night, says the man in the photocopy shop as the machine whirrs and illuminates between them. Hailing and snowing.

What were you doing up?

I came down here. I had something to look after.

She brings this knowledge like a gift from outside to her own office when she trickles in later. Somebody said it hailed at three in the morning downtown.

Where'd you hear this?

At the copy shop.

And the guy in the shop told you this?

Yeah. He said he was down there in the middle of the night.

Sounds like a worried man, says her boss. Nobody comes down to his business at three in the morning, not unless he's worried about something.

75.

A bigger apartment is available upstairs in her building. She goes to look at it. They need more space she's aware. The thin life of a bachelor apartment unsuitable for two really. Her boy is growing.

Number eleven is crowded with someone else's belongings, the two slipcovered, oversize sofas, the table and chairs. There's an inside room in which, the landlord says, the current tenant is asleep. They tiptoe like unwelcome visitors, at least she does. The sink is minute and encased in a tall cabinet: she sees she will have to stand on a stool to do the dishes. Three steps up to the small bath. Perhaps this apartment by the front door belonged to the caretaker once. How bad can it get. She imagines drunks leaning on the intercom at four in the morning.

The apartment is on the northeast corner of the building, looking out over the street. There will be the constant noise of traffic. She meets the tenant who wants to take her old place, who's moving in turn from the front. Musical rooms. It's the noise, the tenant explains, staring. I can't stand it any more.

But you get used to it, right?

Six years and I never got used to it.

She pretends she can adjust to anything but there's her son to consider. She goes to see the child at his father's, sits on a leather sofa, begins seriously to talk about the new apartment, but almost at once her child interrupts.

Yay. Let's move.

She reminds her boy of the noise, the lack of a window in the one small closed-off room, but her child disregards both of these things.

The child's father comes into the room, looks round complacently at his yolk-coloured walls. He's moved himself, she remembers, from the back of his building to its front. She never saw the old place: they weren't speaking then. I had a real freakout when I was trying to decide about moving in here, he says unexpectedly. My friends told me I was crazy. Then I got in here and I was like, Oh yeah. Light. Air.

She wakes far too early the next morning, in her bed in the middle of the room, that she closes like a drawer in the daytime. This one room has been so many different things. Dining room, living room, study, office, bedroom. The simplicity pleases her. Still it's true they have outgrown their current space. Her boy's feet dangling off the edge of the mattress. There will be windows on two sides in the new place, downstairs. Friends can hail them from the street if they want. Traffic swishing outside. Even more places to watch rain as it falls.

76.

Easter. A time of renewal or so it's said, bruited about even, the possibility of growth. So many chances for anniversaries and fresh starts and here is another. She arises from her dented bed filled with resolution. She will sort that errant paper, the piles of it she's been augmenting all year. She will put her taxes into order this time, really. Everything due at the library will be returned, all the languishing dry cleaning rescued, perhaps she will even begin cleaning for their move. The sills and lintels can't accumulate much dust in a month, can they? It isn't too early to wipe down her fridge now, surely?

And all this virtue deserves its reward. She will actually find lingerie this time, not just poke dispiritedly amongst the piles before giving up and going away again. Sets of it, in cotton candy colours: pink sherbet, lavender, innocent blue. She will shop for candy too, the good kind: dark chocolate Easter eggs, pretend carrots in a twist of orange foil.

What about music? She hasn't bought any in years, it's a disgrace. Perhaps she'll even find a suit, a new suit for Easter, now that would be nice. Why she's got so much to do.

The sky outside, what she can see of it from her window, abets her in these fine resolutions. It is blue and strewn with fat tufts of cumulus. They move in a lazy panorama, not hurrying.

But what's this? When she glances at the sky again the white has begun to silt in, filling up the cracks between clouds. The sun recedes behind these wispy layers, a faraway friend getting smaller, waving, waving helplessly. Mouthing advice. Soon rain will come, listen to what it wants, do its bidding.

77.

Everything would be perfect if only. This time it's a walk in the green, but the park at the end of the block is fenced off entirely. First it was the public washrooms they razed. Then the children's playground attached to the school, chained against weekenders. Finally the block was entirely closed off by a metal grid with a sign on it about how this was being done for her benefit. Improvements. A timeline for the bulldozers to ignore. She sees the dog people behind the fence. They got in somehow. We went to all the planning meetings, her neighbour with the aged Pomeranian explains. We told them the dog park was self-policing.

Did they listen to you?

Of course not.

She writes a letter about how the park is her child's backyard, how they cannot go a season without it. Sends it to the name on the sign. No reply.

78.

The season has changed, not gradually as you'd expect but flipped like a switch, the air so soft now she doesn't even notice the window being open. She's looking after Nurse's dog while Nurse works at the Catholic hospital two blocks away. Saints preserve us. The dog lays his heavy head on her knee and then gives up and goes away again, his paws clicking on the polished wooden floor.

Men go up the stairs and come out the elevator in the building opposite, on the floor above. The floor below is obscured by its overhang, in its turn indifferently dappled by the cling of rain. She makes herself breakfast, makes phone calls, combs out her hair in the bath. She should put on some clothes: this mere towel around her waist isn't decent. Wet hair drips onto the crook of her elbow and down her back.

All of Good Friday's intentions have ebbed away. Yes, she should cycle to the natural-foods co-op for beef and organic butter but it's so far to go, and look, the rain has begun again. It's two-way rain. On the one side she can tell herself it's not much: just get out in it, you won't even notice. On the other she can use it as excuse.

She chooses the latter. Yesterday she walked: to the corner store for a week's worth of heavy groceries, seven oranges, two lemons, two limes. To the usual shops. To the bank and then through the shopping mall on the way home, fingering merchandise she won't buy.

79.

Rain again, spring rain, starting last night as wet slashes to the face, irregular, erratic. She catches one full in the lips as she walks, a promissory note. More to come.

Rain starts this way and builds and by nightfall there is glitter everywhere and the small thick noise of its falling. Instead of going out into rain she falls asleep. She wakes often in the night: the air is warmer than she is used to, the quilt heavy on her. Nurse's dog, here still, restless, thumping.

By morning rain has resolved itself into silence. The coating of it on the glass opposite. She's lost her hat somewhere, she can't really go out. Not unless she wants to get wet, with her wanton hair.

80.

Sunshine today. The two of them late again, they're late, they're incredibly late as always. Back to work, back to school, back to the packed lunches and the search for containers, back to the tightness at the back of the throat, forward and back, unraveling. Shuttle. The sky clear as far as the eye can see. It's as if it never rained, not once in their lives. Forget me blue.

81.

This morning she wakes to rain. Cars outside swish through the wet. Will she ride? She has a tight black skirt that cleaves to her hips. The amount of her earnings, gathered in preparation for tax time, astounds her. It comes to her with equal astonishment that she has survived the year. Downstairs in her apartment building is a free shelf, offering up the humblest of discards: dented saltshakers and flimsy plastic dishracks, dollar store discards she discovers anew with cries of internal triumph. And all the while she has been offering up these enormous sums, as she sees it now, to lawyers. In trust.

The rain gives a luminous almost beautiful quality to the yellow lamps shining opposite. There are so many different colours of grey. One so pallid as to be practically negligible, the sky holding rain ready to drop. One dark and stone-coloured. A handful shot through with other colours: a pale flashing kind of lavender, the dark slatey blue of night coming on, even white turning up at the edges, like particoloured covers.

82.

They turn into the city (they become part of the city, they enter into it, this enterprise) on a blue day. Here is puffiness, cloudsful, in the sky. Here is surprised sudden summer. How she drinks up these unpredictably dry days. The sun, far above, impersonally caressing them.

How it all begins to change. How the sky grows dirty with it, like a cloth soiled from cleaning: an imperceptible then overlaid filthy grey. A creeping darkness clouds her in, outside, and then the sentinel drops. Meek they are, the Uriah Heeps of rain.

Us?

Oh nothing.

And the rain, murmuring as if to itself: Don't fuss, mustn't grumble, no, not at all, not a thing, I'll just fall here.

And here and here and here. Like armies or termites they count on being ignored until they can overwhelm. And thus the rain comes, finally, with great violence. The people cluster in doorways and under overhangs, helpless and uncertain. An incidental sorority. The girls in white fluffy summer skirts and little flat shoes. Their small shirts and smaller undershirts. The boys' hoods, the last resource of the wetted, flimsy and inadequate. The people who believed, faithful & betrayed. Wet bounces off the pavement, diagonal slash of water-filled sky, repeat, lose count, overwhelm. A man in a white shirt, soaked to the waist, walks for his car gesturing before him with a small black device. A dowser, a blind man.

The next day: la-la-la sunny, like it never rained.

83.

In the grassy pocket park by the market, overlooking the inlet, a sidewalk preacher shouts his wares. She wanders over possessed.

Nobody wants to listen to you, she shouts, standing in front of him. He controls a wince, but can't refrain from turning slightly, cushioning himself. How much easier to shout than to be shouted at! She is invincible. She goes on and on, matching his every word.

Later, back at the house, S's neighbour out walking her dog. The neighbour stops to talk. She confesses what she did.

Mm. Did you ask him how long he's been doing this?

She didn't ask him a thing.

Ask him how many people he's converted. Then, after he tells you, tell him he might want to consider a different approach.

84.

Times she misses M. An ache she doesn't want to admit even to herself. So many things tainted now, the feel of M's body in the bed next to hers (tightly clasp) overlaid with their last fight. No bed or body to regret now. M reading reports on the couch. The back of her neat, shorn head above a polo collar. What little is left.

85.

Rain again. How summer isn't coming. The afternoon sun, golden, shafting in at a slant. And these puddles lying cross-ways on the road, deep and still. Take a memo, Miss Jones. Let it run as follows: There was rain today, there will be rain tomorrow.

Slashes on the windowpane. Dribbles on the fall. Gloomy morning, gloomy noontime, gloomy day with no hint of what is to come. The future. Will it be warm and sunny again? Or bloody like this forever?

Cutting bread and then, sharply, skin. Red speckles on the wrap, on the bread. Spotted.

Rain starts up again in the afternoon. The sound of rain a thousand shushes, a phalanx of Spanish soldiers: sssss. The blood slows, thickens, clots.

86.

When something is bad there comes a time when she needs it. When that sudden sick feeling in the stomach, that sudden gut sock, that sudden drop is like manna. When she doesn't feel right unless she is reeling from another awful revelation. The poison like milk. She sucks it down from a tube and when the tube is taken away without warning, without notice she feels a sudden irrational sense of loss and panic as she blunders in its wake. The rain starts and she doesn't even have sense to cover herself or get out of the way. She stumbles and lurches a great foolish baby, half-skinned, only partially formed.

She tells herself she can get used to the repeated stupid appearances at court, to the horrible accusations, to the looming up, apologetic but determined, of the next officer. This one, at the airport, enforcing an access order nobody was trying to evade. Your ex-wife, he'll say, trying. She'll interrupt: my wife. Might as well claim it for what it is, make the worst case possible. It's a strategy, like chemotherapy.

She congratulates herself on perfecting her response to strangers who mention her marriage. Universally appropriate, she'd like to think. Wry smile. Oh that, she says. Oh her. Like it's a joke, as if it matters that little to her. Inside she's seething as usual, pot on the boil. The roiling, though she'd never acknowledge it, feels a little bit comforting, a little bit like something she knows.

She's longing to talk about it, to go over it again & again like the tongue goes back to a bad tooth, but she thinks it's only decent to pretend. A bad relationship, she tells herself sagely, everyone's had them. So we were married. So what. Lots of people get married. Lots of times it doesn't work out. The platitudes ring hollow. Secretly she feels her loss is tragic: singular & profound. Secretly she understands: this dissolution is a puzzle she is required to solve. A labyrinth within whose painted lines she consents to remain. Who did what to whom. Who was wrong, who was beyond the pale (M, of course, it's obvious, can't everyone see that?), whether in fact she was to blame. In any way. Whether she had been herself, or someone worse. And how exactly it all went wrong, at what moment their marriage stopped being a container with a few insignificant cracks, when it turned into a casualty. Could no longer hold water. These are questions she will have to answer, to somebody's satisfaction. Hers maybe.

She was so surprised when she saw a labyrinth for the first time: no maze of walls but simply a circle traced on the floor of a church hall, infinitely looping back on itself. She learned then that a labyrinth uses nothing to keep you in, except for your own steps stuck to the pattern.

Nurse stretches out a hand, takes hers, touches the circlet on her third finger. Why do you still wear this, Nurse asks. The answer obvious, to her at least. Because I'm still with M. Only half here. Nurse tucks her in, brings her drinks. She should tell her, say: You know this relationship - significant pause - Isn't Going Anywhere. But she doesn't. Too cruel. A different kind of cruelty, sin of omission, what she's doing now. Back to health. Mum's the word on the nights she and Nurse are apart. Nights she can't sleep, thinking of M.

So many betrayals. Blood under the bridge as her boss would say.

87.

Today rain only threatens. The newspaper says it will come later. Speckles on the glass: ghosts of old dirt or the precursor of things to come, it's hard to say.

Nurse I'm sick. Take my temperature. Intubate me Nurse. Nurse, feel my heart. Right here. Is it beating? How strong is the pulse, Nurse? How much time do I have left?

Nurse take me to your kind glass-walled condo. Carry me inside, in your strong arms. Stagger under my weight. I need looking after, like a baby. I picked you for a reason. Can't you see I'm sick, can't you see what's wrong with me? Can't you tell? Bring the cart. Don't send for the technician. I need you.

Is there anything you need, Nurse asks, passing the bed where she lies. The tall bed on its risers, in the tiny room. The chocolate comforter. Anything I can get you.

No. I'm fine, she says, and turns her face, resolute, to the wall.

88.

She imagines herself in another world. Downstairs. How their surroundings will shape them, how they will expand once they have the space to do so. She'll buy furniture, she swears, she'll look on Craigslist, maybe she'll meet someone, when she goes to look at that midcentury sofa. Someone attractive. Maybe someone who doesn't know about her, about her past, about all her mistakes. She'll paint. She hasn't painted but she can, why not, there's no law, nothing to stop her. In this eternally damp weather it'll take a long time to dry but it doesn't matter, she'll keep the big windows she saw along one wall open, she'll let it cure, or whatever it is paint does. The hardware store will know, they'll sell her some paint that's good for kids, that won't kill them with its fumes. She'll paint a nice, rosy pink, salmon-coloured, so everything gets a warm glow. That'd be nice. Or, no, blue. Tiffany blue, that's it. Her new place will look exactly like a jewel box, the kind you open with trepidation and delight. She'll be expensive, that's it. No greys. Nothing dark. Nothing to remind her of rain.

89.

Today it rained. Yesterday it rained. The day before it
rained.

She stares out unseeing. Behind her she can feel the weight
of the future pressing down on the back of her neck. Have
to call. Need to fix. Wipe and wrap. Her favourite word,
organize. So often anticipated, so never happening.

I'm moving, but I'm still here, she writes her friend finally,
via email. Her friend, her brief ex. The only one who ever
said: I'm getting a desk.

What for? Her ex was a chef, all she needed was a kitchen.

For you. So when you come here, you can write.

Tomorrow it will rain again, she wants to tell her. The day
after, more rain. And you know how it is: each day the rain

ends up being different. Sullen rain. Rain that leaks out of the sky, like an orgasm out of a rock. Mean. Thin. Cold. Rain that lets go. Rain that opens up like a sluice, like internal organs sliding free. Slop and slip. Rain that starts, and stops, and starts again, and peters out, and finally whips itself into a . . . no. Rain that never commits. Rain that should be committed, it's so crazy.

I'm fine, she ends finally. How are you?

90.

She stares at the screen for so long her foot goes to sleep. When she gets up she lurches across the floor like Frankenstein's monster. Frankenstein is the doctor, which is easy to forget.

She's weary of the confessional. Can't she get up off her knees now? It's not like she doesn't have plenty of other things to do. Moving day a faroff train with its single purposeful light bearing down. And her, stuck on the crossing with taped-together boxes.

Just let me get this stuff.

She's waiting for phone calls or to make them. For once she hasn't planned anything. She'd better start cleaning. She'd better start a lot of things. She's always hated moving. Begin packing things she needs between now and then, and later go helplessly through boxes trying to find them? Or wait until the last minute, keeping out everything she might possibly need, and do it in a rush and forget things and pack them sloppy so she can't figure out where anything is when she needs it later? The jumble box, the last one, into which you thrust everything that remains in despair, and then keep on a shelf for years or decades, until the next time you have to look in.

She'll need to make a bunch of phone calls. She'll call her father. He can't help but he listens. She'll go to the neighbours' wedding. They didn't invite her but it's fine, it's casual. Time like a tap: so much, suddenly cut to nothing. This weekend will be different though. Not her usual Saturdays and Sundays, the leaden weight of days undone, followed by the inevitable last-minute panic.

Believe it or not at half past six it was beautiful out here. Beautiful. Now the sky is filling up, cloudy and white. The colour of the day leached away bit by bit, turned down by degrees. Don't forget. Need a coat.

91.

Monday dawns unsettled. Streaks on the windowpane, dribbles on the fall. All weekend it's been raining off and on and then when she gets outside finally nothing but glorious sun for miles. She and her friend Trouble go shopping.

This dress looks okay, she says, pulling it on over her own clothes.

It's twenty dollars, Trouble replies. You can't afford not to buy it.

She and Trouble are well-worn, so much so even they get the joke. Trouble buys everything, she nothing.

Nurse buys a suit to take her to the formal dinner. A man with a leer attempts to pick them both up. She's never had this happen before although she's heard of it, everyone has. She guesses Nurse must be cute in guys' eyes: first time for that. Another reason they don't belong together, Nurse and her. Same sign, semaphore, washroom symbol.

After the dinner rain begins to spatter. The diners hurry to their cars in their formal attire. The women's spindly shoes and the dresses that don't keep them warm.

I had something like that happen once, Trouble tells her when she confesses how much she liked the man with the leer. I wanted the guy so bad I couldn't even walk straight. He was mildly brain-damaged from sniffing glue, and he smelled. It's cuz I was ovulating.

Oh. Turns out she's ovulating too.

92.

Today it will rain. Showers, tapering to more showers.

Yesterday was barely raining. Even though rain covered the tops of puddles in a series of circles, even though the surfaces it touched had reluctantly turned, their pale aspect becoming dark and saturated, there was a lightness to rain. Rain hadn't dug in, taken hold. Rain was liquid rather than solid. She could slip through rain, in her straw hat, without worry. Rain barely touched her.

She is like this with M now. She doesn't turn a hair or rather a hair doesn't tighten to a curl at the thought of M. It has taken a whole year and more. Without a qualm she reports the date of her separation for tax purposes, answers whoever asks.

It's moving that unmoors her. She shouts at her child who's desultorily packing a hundredweight of small plastic parts.

Washes the walls until the water in the pail cools, turns muddy and opaque. She's gone down another dress size, the number a ridiculous one. When this happens she watches what she eats, but in reverse. She looks for the foods highest in fat, the dense kind filled with calories. Spies a bit of pudge spilling over her belt, now. Good.

93.

It's been raining now for days, the rain of spring, cherry blossoms still lining the gutter. On a white-blossom apple tree near the elementary school, one branch sprouting pink among its paler fellows. She pauses, looks up. Can this be nature, or graft?

She gets on the bus with her son. They cross the bridge, go up and over the hill, and descend into the cove. Before them ferries move across the water, melting into the grey dissolving sky. Sea reaches up, its boundaries unstable, for the water that rains down on it. Once on the island they don't even go down to the beach, her Island friend, another single mother, and her. The children are downstairs playing in the damp, their voices muffled. Their mothers huddle under the eaves, on the deck, smoking cigarette after cigarette. Futile puffs. Glasses of wine. The next day, back in Horseshoe Bay, a bus driver taking his break turns the pages of a newspaper. It's still raining.

Everything turns foggy. It's hard to see very far. She loves and hates this cotton batten existence. Like living inside a quilt, buffered. Untouched, unspoken, undelivered, unmoved. Inside the rooms where rain doesn't go she shakes off her lethargy, speaks crisp words into the phone. Outside rain waits for her and everyone else, patient. Rain older than time, made today, somewhere in between, but fated always to cover them.

94.

On the day she removes it rains. She rises with the sound twisted into her waking in the night. Her body hobbled. So much to be done. Outside rain falls heedless.

The new apartment's inner room is beautiful and serene, quietly lit. The outer room large and blighted by the roar and rush of cars on the street before her. She can see people walking by, under the windows, their heads level with the ivy twined outside the glass. It's just as she imagined, only more so.

Her mattress, too big for the new frame, curls up supine. She lies there unable to sleep for hours. At first light she is awake again, suddenly, like a cat.

Some showers, the report says. Outside it is grey.

Some people pass, carrying umbrellas. Now will you be-

lieve in weather? In its permanence, rain's duration, the
span of years?

95.

In her experience bitterness has a flavour. A quick sharp taste in the mouth, like a little stab. Sugar's opposite. Times she can still savour it, if that's the word. When the police call or, even better, visit. Lucky for her she works in a small office, knows everybody. Someone's good taste. Times she tells her story again, willing herself to tell it straight, this time, ha ha. Not the same flavour as rain, that bitterness, not at all. Rain blossoms, the wet a tiny explosion bursting across lips and teeth, and then the taste of dust afterwards. The dust rain carries, that it brings from above, best not considered too closely.

She'd like not to think too much. That would be nice. She'd like to be happy although it seems the only way to do that is to forget. Forget all the things they said to each other, forget all the cruel words and reproach. How could you. Why can't we. Remember the good things, the good times. Just one problem, one question. Were there any?

96.

Somewhere below or beside her the sound of an alarm clock's hootenanny chorus. Sound hard to locate exactly, rising in this warren.

Afternoon. A neighbour's computer kicks into life with noisy beeps and trills. Leaning on the buzzer outside, the same woman who's accosted her before, at the same door. Another day, same sodden set to her clothes, and still visibly drugged, flesh having given up the job. The moral problem of admittance. The woman's plaint: I can't get in. She gives the woman the same lecture at which the young woman returns the same acquiescent monosyllables. Yep. Okay. Sure. So many hectoring words the young woman has to pretend to absorb, for the sake of whatever it is she wants.

At night the sound of people rises outside her windows. They are talking loudly as if in their own homes. Perhaps they are in their own homes six metres from hers in the next building or upstairs, big sash windows thrown open to the cold.

A young woman's laugh, a young man's excited lengthy explanation. Song rises in dissonant chorus from a group of people swaying down the street. Gradually dies away. She sleeps through the small hours, perfectly content. There was a time when she would wake in the night and hear the gasp of women above, their keening and urgency. Now nothing.

Each hour gradually comes to life in a rising wall of sound. At five a.m. there is perfect stillness, broken only by the occasional car passing on the street outside. By six the sound of engines rushing by has become intermittent. The cars always have somewhere to go and never want to stop.

By seven the traffic has begun to coalesce into a steady stream: droplets of water joining together to form a spotty rain, then a torrent.

97.

Today it rains in stops and starts. There's a lot of it on her ride in but she hardly cares. She is wearing the perfect outfit: a high-waisted woolen pencil skirt, close black cotton shirt, black thigh-highs and little stiletto boots. Women like her have a faith in correct attire bordering on the alchemical. Only find the perfect dress and the rest of the world will resolve itself as in your dreams. Lovers at your feet. Jobs for the taking. Travel, gifts, your heart's truest desire. Sunny skies forever.

After she gets to the office she and her boss drive out to the warehouse in the low-lying part of town. Richmond is flat and held in by banked earth: a few more years and it'll be under water. She carries boxes of books in her perpendicular heels. Then back to the office to unload. The rain has sputtered to an occasional dribble, not even worthy of the office umbrella. She packs books and makes up parcels and later rides to the bookstore where one of their authors is launching his latest book. After it's over she walks to a restaurant with her editor friends. Cherry blossom swirls underfoot. Crushed and banked.

I go in there once a year, the vegetarian confesses as they pass the hamburger stand. For the meat.

She regards the woman with new respect.

The next morning the dark grey stains on her boots won't come off, not even when she scrubs them with a cloth. Permanently marked from their passage. Familiar, that.

98.

In her city they are proud of rain or rather proud of themselves for surviving it. They have two modes: the amnesia of summer, and then the self-conscious display of their hardihood in the face of intolerable odds in the interminable wet wintertime. They like to be noticed & admired. They appreciate your marvel although everything must take place without overt acknowledgement. That's their sweet silent way.

So they never speak of how it grows into them, this rain. The familiar scent of old mildew that curls up from the collar of a coat wet again for the millionth time. The drip they come to listen for, in the big pipe outside the bedroom window as they lie. Supine again. The blind panic of January, when they swear to themselves they can't take it for one more second, and then February's deathlike resignation. The annual suicide of their hopes: rain remains, sun gone, never again to shine.

Instead, they pretend to hover above these heavenly annoyances. It's their gift, along with a coloured rolled mat they carry everywhere and that green liquid in a plastic cup they tote from place to place. She watches them. She's one herself, after all. No need to set herself apart. Raises her own green-brimmed glass.

99.

First weekend in May. Back in her usual room: a long, low-slung one, under the eaves, braced with roughly-hewn tree trunks. Outside a porch, and the roof, extending far beyond with its massive beams.

On her first visit the lodge's keeper got up, at dinner, to tell the story of how the lodge burnt to the ground in 1985. The family, he said, stood and watched. What are we going to do? he asked his father, while the firefighters' hoses still played. The father said immediately: "Rebuild it the way it was, I guess." After all, he pointed out, they know nothing else.

So the son keeps the new lodge. Genial, faintly remote, passing through. Same faces in the lounge from one year to the next. Only the youngsters serving in the dining room differ.

Last year she brought M for the first time. They took the Triumph. On the way back it broke down in the lineup to the ferry. M enraged, she shrugging. What do you expect. Their roles, familiar now.

This weekend is grey, colder than she's used to. In past years she's plunged breathless into the seawater pool, sunned on the rocks. Not this time. The other guests miss the promise of warmth. How nice it would be, in summer, everyone says, wandering over the rocky face. The people she knows vaguely from past years, without knowing their names.

There's a type who comes here, to the point. The man is older, faintly amused, as is the woman. They've stayed to-gether. They're comfortable, quiet, they like a glass of wine, she drinks a lot of tea. There's an allowance and elasticity. Something to teach her. Maybe. Here she is, fifth wheel, sore thumb. By herself in the hot tub, by herself on the bal-cony. Everyone else accompanied, by friends if not mates.

It comes to her that she is lonely. She rests her arms on the rail, feeling the familiar weight in the middle of her body, the heavy sag of it under her skin. She'll spring back, won't she?

While she is standing there the view of the sea, beyond the big sloping slab of rock descending to the shore, begins to dull and haze over. The blue of the forested slopes down the island lightens to grey. The line between ocean and sea has snapped: in its place, an inexact boundary blurs the division.

There come to her softly, like the softest little steps of the smallest tiptoeing person, the first tiny sounds of rain. How hesitantly they come across the water, on this quiet shore. Deer grazing on the slopes. Bunnies hopping along the grass. The quiet of rain quietly beginning to fall.

Acknowledgements

While this novel takes its inspiration from the lives we all lead day to day and year to year, it is a work of fiction and the characters are in no way meant to represent real people. Real people did, however, have a great deal to do with any art in the narrative that follows. I would like to thank, first and foremost, my writing group for seeing this book before I did: Mindy Abramowitz, Kate Bird, Shannon Underwood, Rhonda Waterfall, and others. Further thanks are due to Archer Pechawis, Peter Nosco, and Carson, for being a ray of light. And finally, my favourite gang of Thugs: Malcolm Sutton, for thoughtful editing and design; Hazel Millar, for publicity; and Jay Millar, for the leap of faith.

About the Author

Rhodes Scholar Carellin Brooks is the author of *fresh hell: motherhood in pieces* (2013), *Wreck Beach* (2007), and *Every Inch a Woman* (2005). She edited the anthologies *Carnal Nation*, with Brett Josef Grubisic, and *Bad Jobs*. Winner of the Books in Canada Student Writing Award for poetry (1993), the Cassell/Pink Paper Lesbian Writing Award for non-fiction (1994), and the Institute for Contemporary Arts New Blood Award for prose (1995), Brooks lives and works in Vancouver, where she was born.

Colophon

Distributed in Canada by the Literary Press Group www.lpg.ca
Distributed in the United States by Small Press Distribution www.
spdbooks.org

Shop online at www.bookthug.ca

BOOK
PRODUCTION
WAR ECONOMY
STANDARD

Edited for the press by Malcolm Sutton
Copy edited by Ruth Zuchter
Designed by Malcolm Sutton
Typeset in Yoga